ANYWHERE WITH YOU

WITH YOU SERIES | BOOK TWO

BRITNEY KING

WWW.BRITNEYKING.COM

COPYRIGHT

Hot Banana Press

Cover Design by Britney King

Cover Image by by Matthew Henry

Copy Editing by Literary Agent Rogena Mitchell-Jones

Proofread by Proofreading by the Page

First Edition: 2015

ISBN: 978-0-9966497-1-1 (Paperback)

ISBN: 978-0-9966497-0-4 (All E-Books)

britneyking.com

For those who know wanderlust in their bones.
Their eyes made of love,
Hearts of gold.
To those who find their way home again.

ANYWHERE WITH YOU

BRITNEY KING

JACK

I COULDN'T STAY.

AVE YOU EVER held something so beautiful you wanted to hang onto it—and yet at the same time, put it aside just for fear of using it up? I have. It's like that uncle of yours who owns several amazing classic cars, and while he tinkers with them daily—he rarely actually takes them out for a drive. Or—your Grandma and her fine china, which only sees the light of day on special occasions. Or maybe it's that little black dress you keep hanging in the back of your closet despite the fact that you haven't worn it in a decade because you assure yourself you'll fit back into one of these days.

That's how I felt about her. She was all of the things I mentioned above—compiled into one really amazing person. And I was afraid that I'd use her up.

Over time—I might've learned that there was so much more where that came from—if only I'd just kept looking. But that's not what happened in South America. Basically, you could say I choked. And I'm not one who chokes. Yet, with her—it happened. With her... it always happens.

I'd spent such a long time trying to locate Amelie and

traveling to find her. And then, when I did—well, it was beyond anything I could have expected. She was the same— only better. She was still as captivating as ever, smarter, and worldlier, too. In a sense, we were both better than the last time we'd spent time together. Just not good enough, I guess.

There's also the fact that I left in the shittiest way possible. Unexpectedly and without notice. Which if you're going to leave a woman, really, it's the best—if not *the only* way to go about doing it. Before you hate me too much, let me say this—I did at least leave a note.

If I were to try and explain to you then *why* I left, I couldn't. Mostly because I'm not certain I even really knew myself. But I know now.

It's been two years since I walked out of that hotel room leaving Amelie lying naked tangled up in the mess we'd made only hours before. As I studied the way the early morning light poured in through the balcony doors and filtered itself over her tanned, bare skin, I ran my fingers through her hair and watched as she stirred a little. If I remember correctly, and I do, because I've thought back over those moments thousands of times, probably at least once every day since that morning, I remember she smiled in her sleep. She was happy. Too damned happy. And maybe that was the problem.

I do recall willing her to wake, willing her to get up, to ask me just what in the hell I was doing. But she didn't. She merely sighed, pulled the covers up to her chin, and rolled over onto her stomach. So I kissed the top of her head, placed the note on the bedside table, and that was that.

Two days later, I received an email.

To: Jack Harrison

From: Amelie Rose

Subject: You're an asshole.

Jack,

From here on out, leave me alone.

Life is better that way.

Amelie

It was just like Amelie to want the last word, but I wasn't the kind of guy, not then anyway, to let her have it.

To: Amelie Rose

From: Jack Harrison

Subject: Tell me something I don't know…

Dear Amelie,

I can't. It's against my nature.

I truly am sorry for leaving the way I did.

I just had to get back...

Love,

Jack

When I wrote that email, I expected a response. Basically, I wanted more from her. I wanted her to tell me that we could make it work this time. I wanted her to fight. I wanted her to tell me to go to hell—that I was wrong to leave. And in a sense, I guess she did—because I didn't see or hear from her again for nearly two years.

AMELIE

HERE COMES TROUBLE.

J was already in a bad mood. For starters, I'd overslept, my cab showed up late, and security lines were backed up—all factors that not only lent to my crappy mood but factors that also caused me to miss my flight. Then, as if that weren't shitty enough, the airline informed me I'd have to wait another six hours before they'd have room on another flight. A flight, mind you that would get me *not* to my destination—but closer than I was currently. The attendant assured me her offer was better than my current predicament, her tone clearly reveling in my misery. So instead of one flight, I'd now need to take two, in addition to the six-hour layover I was about to endure. I told the indifferent airline attendant that I'd accept the offer—because, after all, what other choice did I have?

"You could always stay here." She offered with a smile. They must train them that way, I thought. It's as though they hold a special class or something on just how to serve the right amount of passive-aggressiveness. I wanted to ask as much, to find out where she learned to be so pleasantly rude. Instead, I simply smiled, shook my head, and offered my best thank you, but no thank you expression. I let my smile fade, just to drive home the point that she hadn't completely won, and I reached down and grabbed the handle to my carry-on, the only luggage I travel with, which had, of course, fallen over at my feet, and walked away with my tail between my legs. Thoroughly exhausted, I searched for the respite of caffeine. I'd already decided the only thing that could possibly save me at this point was the combination of coffee and work—of which I had no shortage of to catch up on. It was just that I'd hoped to catch up on in the air.

And, anyway, not only was I not in the mood for a fight—I'd had enough of that in the past twenty-four hours—but also I wasn't particularly in a hurry to actually reach my destination. Nonetheless, had I been in any kind of rush, it would have been a losing battle anyhow, as it happened to be the busiest travel day of the year—the day before Thanksgiving. I was traveling to see my part-time lover, full-time pain in the ass, also known as Ian. We'd had it out the night before, which was in part the reason for my tardiness this morning. I hadn't slept much at all—and I certainly hadn't planned on falling asleep when I did. The trouble was that Ian had been pressuring me for a larger commitment than I was willing to give. Worse yet, Ian was also my boss. I know, I know. It was stupid. Really, really stupid. I mean what kind of idiot gets involved with their boss? Well, this kind. Apparently.

In my defense, though, he was not my boss at the time we began sleeping together. He was actually my boss's boss. Which probably sounds worse, I get it, but let me assure you —it wasn't. At least back then, there was a buffer. And honestly, I didn't plan to sleep with him. Like most mistakes, it just sort of happened. My heart was broken and Ian just so happened to be the first right—yet very wrong—thing to show up in my life. My boss—at the time—and the editorial team I worked with had gone out to celebrate the wrapping of the magazine's latest issue. Despite the fact that I wasn't keen on going anywhere after my latest romantic debacle, my boss had demanded that everyone be in attendance. Her boss, a.k.a Ian, had flown in, and one drink wouldn't kill anyone, she'd assured me.

At any rate, she made it clear that it was a mandatory meeting and that my latest crisis, as she called it, was no excuse not to be in attendance. Little did she know, I actually liked the idea of having a drink. Or six. Minus the going out part.

Still, to prove a point, I waltzed into that hotel lobby looking about like I felt. Run down and out of fucks to give. I moseyed up to the group and took my place at the table. Then I promptly ordered a vodka and tonic and chased that one down with a few more. By my fourth drink, not only was I the life of the party, I was the boss's *boss's* new favorite person. This one has talent, I can tell, I remembered he'd remarked as he ordered another round.

Somewhere around drink five and a half, Erica, my assistant, grabbed my elbow, led me out of the hotel, and onto the street where she'd attempted in vain to put up with my drunken nonsense while simultaneously trying to wave down a cab. Perhaps if she would've succeeded, or if I would have left sooner or maybe hadn't consumed so many drinks, my life would be less of a mess right now. But she didn't succeed, and I did manage to once again not only drink myself under the table but everyone else, too. And so, as it turned out, Ian intercepted us out on the street.

"Wait up," I remember him calling out, the expression he wore one of relief.

I eyed him up and down as he headed toward us. I liked the way he smiled warmly as he slowly jogged in my direction. Maybe I'd hoped this would happen. Maybe a part of me had wanted him to follow us out. Thinking back to the person I was then and the frame of mind I was in—otherwise known as 'after Jack'—I can only assume I was glad to see the tall, tailored suit trotting my way. When he stopped just a few feet shy of me, his deep brown eyes bore into mine. The air was suddenly stagnant. It hurt to breathe. The sounds of the city, of traffic, and of voices laughing and arguing, the coming and going, it all faded into the background, and all I saw was the man standing before me.

"I was afraid I wouldn't catch you," he finally said.

My breath caught at the deep tone of his voice and the words he'd chosen. Of all the words, I thought, he'd picked those. And they were perfect. I didn't know if I wanted to be caught—but I definitely knew a distraction couldn't hurt. Which was partly how I'd found myself in the position I was in. Drunk and being led out of an office party by my assistant. As I considered this, I stumbled on my heel. Erica tightened her grip on my elbow and then released it all together. Whether she was willing to let me fall remained to be seen.

"I wanted to have a word with Miss Rose," he said to Erica, although he didn't take his eyes off of mine.

Then he turned. "About the upcoming issue… and the changes…"

Erica looked at me, but only for a second, and then back at him. I watched as she rubbed her lips together, her signature sign she made whenever she was unsure.

"I think Lisa was asking after you," he said. "And no worries, I'm an expert at hailing cabs. I can take it from here." His voice was calm, his words smooth and demanding, just the way I liked them. His demeanor reminded me of Jack. Or at least the Jack I thought I'd known.

"You'll be ok?" Erica asked squeezing my forearm.

I smiled. Or at least I think I did. I must have given some

reassurance because I watched as she walked away. My memory remembers her turning just outside the hotel doors and mouthing the words 'don't do it.' Maybe that's just wishful thinking though because, at any rate, I certainly didn't listen, and the two of us had never discussed the matter again.

Ian placed his hands on my shoulders and squeezed. "I actually do have a few things I'd like to discuss with you." He searched my eyes, for what I wasn't sure. "First, though, perhaps some water." He released my shoulders, took my hand in his, and pressed a room key into it. "Room 802."

I don't recall if I said anything, but I think I must have laughed because he steadied me on my feet, leaned in, and whispered harshly in my ear, "I'm not kidding here. I'll see you in twenty minutes. You won't let me down, will you?" He smiled. "I'm counting on you…"

I liked that he was serious. Finally, here was a man who knew what he wanted and asked for it.

"See you soon." I swallowed.

And see him I did.

He opened the door to his room just as I was about to turn to go. He must have sensed my hesitation to knock, to actually go through with meeting him in his room. But five vodka tonics had gotten me there, and so far, they hadn't been enough to override my good senses, so by the time he opened the door, I remember feeling relieved. He'd started this. I would finish it. He took me by the wrist and gently pulled me inside. It was the beginning of a secret. And the end of me.

He had a towel wrapped around his waist, his body still moist from the shower. The muscles in the upper half of his body glistened and I couldn't help but stare. He was more toned than I'd thought with clothes on, his build tall and lean. He had a runner's body. But even if he hadn't—I'm not sure it would've made any difference. "I brought a drink up for you," he said slipping my feet out of my heels, trailing the back of his hand up my thigh. "Vodka and tonic, right?"

"Yes," I said.

And that was that.

I recall him making love to me tenderly as though I were a present he'd been waiting to unwrap. It was different than I'd expected it to be, more calculated—which, I would soon learn, pretty much summed up Ian Larson.

～

"Why didn't you tell me?" I demanded two days later, shortly after I'd gotten word that my boss was being promoted, and Ian was stepping into her position in the interim—until a replacement was found.

He crossed his new corner office and stood before me. "I did tell you... Perhaps you were just too inebriated to remember."

I knew he hadn't told me. And I was pretty sure he knew that I knew he hadn't told me. "No. I wasn't. And, no, you didn't."

"Look, I'm sorry. Maybe there was a misunderstanding but—" He paused, walked over to the door, and closed it. He turned to me. "But it doesn't change anything." He shrugged. "No one has to know what we do."

"What we did."

His jaw hardened, but he recovered quickly. "That's up to you."

"You're my boss. You knew you were my boss... and you still seduced me."

"And I recall you liking it very much."

I sighed. "It was unethical."

"It's funny you should mention that, Amelie. Because I

hardly remember your actions that night, both before or after, being anything but ethical."

I swallowed hard. He had me and he knew it. "Well, it won't happen again."

"Perhaps not. But at any rate, I'm glad you're here. Actually, I've been meaning to speak to you about something—" Ian drew in a long breath and slowly let it out. "I really think if you play your cards right, that you have a real shot at this position," he said using his oversized hands to elaborate by motioning around the office. "But at the very least, it would require a little pleasantry. You do know how to be nice, right, Amelie?"

I walked past him toward the door. "I wouldn't count on it," I said stopping just outside the doorframe.

But two very long days later, I found myself back in his bed. And as I recall, neither of us were very nice.

3

JACK

DID SHE KNOW I LOVED HER?

*I*f you were to ask me if I believe in fate, I would tell you that no, I do not. I believe in making things happen. I believe in preparation, in showing up, and playing full out. But I guess if there is such a thing, what happened that day at the airport was as close to fate as it comes.

You see, the truth is, I had been plotting how to 'run in' to her for a few weeks by that point. I'd perused the likes of Google, and then the brilliance of social media, to try to find out as much as I could about her whereabouts and what she'd been up to. But then I decided that 'accidental run-ins' are for pussies. If I wanted to see her, well, then she should know it. It wasn't exactly like she didn't *not* want to see me, and honestly, I missed her. Probably more than I'd ever missed anyone. Maybe even more than I missed my mother. And she's dead. So that says a lot. What to do about it, though, I hadn't quite figured out. Not the part about my mother, of course. The dead thing tends to figure itself out. I mean the part about Amelie.

So I hadn't figured it out, and I don't believe in fate, and yet it happened. Whatever you want to call it—fate, serendipity, the stars aligning—your guess is as good as mine.

But there she was.

The day before Thanksgiving. McCarren Airport. Terminal Two. I was headed home from Vegas following a mostly successful business trip when I saw her. It was the legs I noticed first. Skirt. Expensive heels. Typical Vegas. I hadn't necessarily been looking for a skirt. But I hadn't *not* been looking either. And what better place than a crowded airport in which one was about to be trapped in a metal vessel hurling through the air for the better part of three hours to find someone to fill the time with? Anyhow, so there they are—such a great set of legs, and I knew even before I saw her, the owner of them had to be my type. I wasn't usually wrong. She was bent forward rummaging through her bag, her hair, hanging down, covering her face. I watched her for a moment before she sat straight up and her eyes locked on mine. Amelie. Strangely, she was just as—if not more—breathtaking than the last time I saw her. Twenty-five months and four days ago.

I watched her expression change as her mind registered what, or more importantly, whom she was seeing. Judging by the look on her face, I couldn't quite tell if she was indifferent or devastated. She certainly didn't seem happy, that's for sure. I did my best to keep my expression neutral as I made my way over to where she sat.

Stopping just shy of her, I dropped my backpack at my feet.

"Fancy meeting you here," I said, more excitedly than I'd intended.

She stood. "Jack... Wow. What you are you doing here?"

I looked around at the weary travelers as they filed past

us. I paused for a moment before answering. Then I reached in for a hug. Just shy of her ear, I whispered, "What I assume everyone else is doing." I squeezed her tight without letting go right away. She hugged me back and then pulled away as she eyed me up and down.

"You look…"

"Older?"

She smiled though just a little. I noticed it didn't touch her eyes. "Well, that too."

"Oh, you meant sexier. Yeah, I get that a lot."

Amelie rolled her eyes. "I'm sure."

I glanced toward the window where a plane was taxiing in. "So, it looks like we're on the same flight."

She looked over her shoulder toward the gate, and once again, her expression changed. "Oh… no. I just stopped here because I can't seem to find my phone." She motioned toward her bag. "I had it in the cab on the way over—so I know it's here somewhere."

I swallowed hard as the realization that our encounter would be brief sunk in. It took me a second to recover. "Ah. Well, I could call it. You have the same number?"

She nodded slowly and then studied the floor.

I pulled my phone from my pocket and dialed by pressing her name on the screen. Suddenly, I felt her eyes searching mine, but I didn't look immediately look up.

"I'm surprised to see that I'm still on your favorites list," she mentioned, never one to miss a thing.

"Always." I smiled and then my eyes met hers.

She looked away.

"I didn't mean for it to end, you know."

Her phone rang and she reached toward the sound.

"I just had to get back," I told her, trying and failing to get her to look my way.

Amelie didn't respond for several minutes as she messed

around on her newly found phone. Finally, she looked up. "Yeah, I know." She shrugged slightly. "I mean... I understand."

"You do?"

She pursed her lips. "Sure."

"Then why didn't you ever write back... why didn't you call."

"I don't know." She bit her lip. "But I can think of a few reasons."

I waited, but instead of speaking, she shifted and waved me off. "Ah, well, you know... It's all water under the bridge anyhow. That was practically a lifetime ago."

"It was twenty-five months ago. I wouldn't exactly call that a lifetime."

Her face broke into a smile. "Yeah, but who's counting?"

Overhead, I heard my flight being called for pre-boarding.

"Sounds like that's you."

I didn't budge. "I have time."

She shifted backward on her heel. "It was really great to see you, Jack," she said, her voice losing its edge.

I watched as a toddler squirmed just enough to break free from his mother's grasp. Once free, he ran full-speed toward the window. Amelie followed my gaze and I shifted my attention back to her.

"What time does your flight take off?"

She checked the time on her phone and frowned. "About five hours and fifteen minutes from now."

I choked. "What?"

"It's a long story..."

"You couldn't get an earlier flight? I asked, confused. "Where are you headed?"

She shook her head. "Boston."

"Ah." I could tell she didn't really want to expand on the topic so I let it go.

Another call for boarding came overhead.

But as soon as the silence had grown just awkward enough, I realized I had to know. "What's in Boston?"

"A friend."

"I see." I nodded and then studied the pattern on the floor. "Well… that's one lucky friend," I remarked, eventually meeting her gaze.

She smiled. "Something like that."

"I could catch a later flight and wait with you."

"Oh gosh, no. That's crazy," she scoffed.

I reached into my pocket for my boarding pass. "I've been called worse."

"I bet." Amelie grinned and then I watched it fade. Her tone turned serious. "But seriously, no. Go get on that plane. We can catch up later. You should call me some time…"

I waited for her to say something else. Anything else. And when she didn't, I leaned in and hugged her. Then I kissed her cheek and slowly pulled away. "I will," I promised, taking her in. "It was so good to see you. I've really missed you."

She nodded curtly before reaching down for her carry-on. "Happy Thanksgiving, Jack," she said once again meeting my eye.

I reached for her hand, took it in mine, and gave it a squeeze. "Happy Thanksgiving," I whispered.

I gave her one last look up and down. I smiled. So did she.

And then I turned to go.

～

I ACTUALLY HAD BOARDED THAT PLANE WITH THE FULL intention of landing in Texas. I took my seat and stared out the window as the workers scurried around down below. But still, no matter how hard I tried, I couldn't stop my thoughts from drifting back to the encounter with Amelie. My heart raced as I poured back and forth over what I'd said, what I hadn't said, what I should have said, and I just couldn't let it go.

I searched my phone, scanning through the two dozen emails that had landed in my inbox since I'd last checked an hour ago. But they were a blur. Everything was a blur. I couldn't help wanting nothing more than to dial her up right then and there. I wanted to set the record straight. And more than that, I realized I wasn't ready for the conversation to end.

To make matters worse, seated just across the aisle from me were a pair of lovers—honeymooners, I'd guess if I were a betting man. I watched from the corner of my eye as they laughed and kissed, and later, when I looked over, her hands were tangled in his hair. I sighed loudly, I'm sure, and slunk back into my seat. Sitting across from those two for the duration of the flight seemed just about more than I could handle. The girl briefly met my eye. My annoyance only seemed to entice her performance as she began biting at her lover's earlobe. I shot her a 'go to hell' look and shifted in my seat where I did my best to focus on anything but Amelie and the love-fest ensuing around me.

Once I'd just about succeeded, I heard the words that would ultimately change the direction I was headed that day. 'Tell me you love me,' the girl squealed. And just like that, I was out of my seat. For no good reason, and for every good reason. I grabbed my bag from the overhead bin and squeezed through the line of weary passengers trying to board, who unlike me hadn't purchased first class seats.

All I knew was I had to get off of that plane and find her. I had to tell her something—what, I wasn't quite sure—mostly,

I just wanted to hear her voice for a few moments longer. It was ridiculous and rash—but I didn't care.

I'd half expected to see her standing there waiting for me as I deplaned. Only she wasn't. She wasn't at my gate, and once I'd located hers, I found she wasn't there either. Maybe she'd decided to get on another flight. God, I hoped she hadn't decided to get on another flight.

I searched faces through the crowd. The airport was teeming with people. There were so many people. And yet none of them were the one I was searching for. None of them were her.

Eventually, I pulled out my phone and pressed the button to dial her. Seconds that felt like hours later, somewhere just over my shoulder, I heard a phone ring. When I turned toward the familiar sound, there she was. Hands on her hips, a disapproving smile on her face.

"Hey," I called out ending the call. "What the hell? I've been looking all over for you!"

"I can see that." She smirked. "But, damn it, Jack—you should've stayed on that plane…"

I waved my hand in the air. "There will be others."

"Touché," she said as I closed the gap between us.

Amelie studied me for a second, tucked her phone away, and began walking. She quickly picked up her pace, so much so, that I had to hustle to keep up. "So, hold up… you saw that I was searching for you, and you…you just let me keep looking?"

She pressed her lips together and raised her brow. "Yep. And it was pretty fun."

"But how did you know I'd…"

She stopped suddenly and looked from side to side, clearly in search of something. I'd just about bumped into the back of her and nearly tripped in the process of attempting to avoid a collision.

"I know you, Jack," she said as she picked up the pace once again.

I didn't immediately follow. "Wait. Where are we going?"

"Somewhere I can get a drink," she called back over her shoulder.

I cocked my head. "It's not even noon."

She paused then and turned. "My point exactly."

❧

4

AMELIE

ON THE RUN.

*W*hy did he have to get off of that damned plane? Why, oh why, oh why? The last thing I needed on what was already a shitty day was another complication. Yet, sure enough, the complication I hadn't needed showed up in the form of Jack Harrison.

I knew he wouldn't get on that plane. But then he surprised me. And once he did, I'd thought maybe, just maybe, he'd stay. Only, I knew him too well to not stick around and watch it all play out. I needed to see him fly away. I needed to know that my heart was safe again. I needed to be able to breathe with ease. I needed the queasiness to subside.

And then I saw him rush back out. I watched his face search the crowd and his eyes scan the terminal. Seeing him there, knowing he was looking for me, watching his reserved desperation, did nothing to cure my symptoms. So for a little while, I hid.

I didn't want to be found, and yet, at the same time, a part of me did. Ironically, this had always been the premise of our relationship to one another. We'd always played a great game of hide and seek. Catch and release. Eventually, though, after watching his expression change from annoyed to worried to somewhat forlorn, my resolve wore thin, and I let him find me. Which is exactly how and why we wound up there in that airport bar.

For approximately two rounds of drinks—for me anyway—we stuck to safe topics. Work and the weather.

By round three, I'd made my second mistake. Turns out the liquor only further wore down any resolve I might have had left.

It started out innocently enough. "So what are your plans for Thanksgiving?" I casually asked. Mere seconds later, just as it escaped my lips, I realized what a dangerous question it actually was. It was the kind where the rubber sort of meets the road—where I'd find out what was really going on, or more importantly, who was going on in Jack's life these days. It was one of the myriads of methods of finding out if there was someone special in one's life, packaged neatly around the safe topic of holiday plans.

He paused and considered me for a moment before answering. "Maybe you should slow down," he finally remarked as he eyed my half-empty glass.

Little did he know. "I'm good," I said shifting in my seat.

He looked away then. "I'm not sure. I haven't really given it much thought."

He was lying. "Thanksgiving is tomorrow, Jack."

His eyes met mine. "Yeah…"

I searched his face for clues. "That's not like you," I finally said.

"I've never much cared for Thanksgiving." He shrugged. "It's just another day to me."

I picked up my tumbler, took a sip, and sat it back down. "Have we ever spent Thanksgiving together?"

He shook his head. "No," he replied. Then all of a sudden, he grinned. "But we should change that."

"You should come with me," I blurted out without giving the idea much thought. Then I raised my glass once again and gulped down the rest of the vodka tonic.

He tilted his head. "To Boston?"

"Why not?" I shrugged. "It doesn't sound like you have big plans or anything. Plus, there's someone I'd really like you to meet."

I watched as his jaw tightened. It felt like forever before he spoke again. "It sounds serious."

"Oh, I don't know... I just—"

He placed his glass of water down on the table. Hard. "Well, in that case, how could I possibly say no?"

I clapped. "So you'll come?"

Jack's mouth twisted. "I'll fly to Boston with you. Let's start there."

"It's as good as place as any, I guess."

He raised his brow. "I figure someone has to watch your liquor consumption."

I laughed. "Oh, come on. So you're telling me it wasn't your plan all along to get me drunk?"

"Are you drunk, Amelie?" His tone had suddenly turned more serious—if such a thing were even possible.

"Well, no, but—"

His eyes were cold, far off. "Then I guess you have your answer."

As we made our way through the hustle and bustle of the airport from one terminal to the next, Jack rattled on incessantly. In my attempt at sobering up, I mostly let him rant on and on until I finally realized that, true to form, Jack didn't just want to be heard—he wanted to be engaged. Jack needed an opponent in order to play his game. And, eventually, the harder my head pounded, the more each syllable he uttered became like a grinder inside my skull, the more I realized I was no longer in the mood to sit on the bench. I wanted to play.

By the time we'd finally boarded the plane and taken our seats, my patience had reached an all-time low.

"I still don't understand why we couldn't get seats in first class." He huffed.

"Because, for the tenth time, Jack, they're full!"

"Yeah, well, for the eleventh time, I don't like sitting this close to strangers for extended periods of time."

"One, I'm not a stranger. And two, you know what I don't like? Complainers. Three, I'll give you my window seat, just for being such a big baby. Move," I barked as I stood and ushered him to do the same. He shot me a look but stood nonetheless and moved outward into the aisle. As I briskly scooted past him, being in such a confined space, I couldn't help but brush against his body. Maybe it was the alcohol or maybe it was just the sturdiness of him that caught me off guard, but I tripped forward just a little and he caught me by my forearm. For the briefest of moments, I let myself fully lean into him, and I paused inhaling the familiar scent of a man I'd loved and lost and everything in between. But just as soon as I'd leaned in, I pulled away.

"Go!" I demanded. "I hope my seat makes you happy."

"Thank God for small favors." He scoffed, eyeing me sideways.

"I thought you being here was sort of a favor."

He looked taken aback, and if I wasn't mistaken, a tad bit hurt. "Is that what you think? That you're doing me a favor?"

"No. Not really," I relented. "I didn't mean that." I sighed. "Why are we fighting anyway?"

"Funny. You call this fighting?"

"Ok, Mr. Semantics. Why are we arguing?"

"This isn't arguing. This is communicating."

I folded my arms across my chest. "Then maybe we should stop."

"We tried that once. And look how well it turned out."

I titled my head. "No, you tried that once."

"You see, Amelie. Now, this is communicating."

"Well, it's so nice to see you've learned a thing or two."

"Oh, I've learned more than that. You just wait."

I rolled my eyes. "My God, Jack."

"That's exactly what you'll say when I show you."

I shifted away from him. "You're delusional."

"Time will tell." He grinned.

"I'm with someone, Jack."

An older gentleman took the aisle seat and looked from Jack to me, and then back. He nodded at each of us, uttering a word or two of salutation, and then looked away and pulled out a tattered paperback.

"That's never stopped you before," Jack finally said.

"You're an asshole."

"And a delusional one at that."

I shifted my body to further face the old man. "Stop communicating with me. I'm taking a nap." I huffed over my shoulder.

"You two sound like my wife and I." The man smirked. "It'll be thirty-four years next month."

I opened one eye and peeked out. "Oh, we're actually not together."

The man laughed, looking at Jack and then back at me. "Sure you are."

My mouth formed a hard line, but nothing came to mind that seemed appropriate to say, so I left it at that. I was tired of talking, and I even more so, I was tired of men. Mostly, I

27

was tired of having to fight to prove my point. I sat there and attempted to doze off. However, sleep proved elusive, despite the four drinks I'd consumed. All I could think about was how this 'situation' was going to end. I knew I shouldn't have asked Jack to tag along and had I not been a bit inebriated, I probably wouldn't have. But, at the same time, I also knew I couldn't tell him the truth.

I couldn't give Jack Harrison a way in. I couldn't let him think he had a shot at anything more than platonic friendship. Because he didn't have shot. Not again. I had decided then and there, as I watched him get off that plane—even looking as smooth and as handsome as he was—all business —that I wouldn't let myself go down that road this time. After all, I'd been down it one too many times before and I knew full well exactly where it led. And it wasn't anywhere I wanted to go.

Furthermore, the truth was complicated enough—even without speaking it aloud. In part, I'd asked Jack along to shield me from what I knew lay ahead in Boston. But I couldn't tell him that. I couldn't tell him I was afraid of what was to come. And I certainly couldn't tell Jack, without giving him the notion that he had a way in, that I figured having him there would make it all better. So I didn't.

If only, though—I hadn't figured wrong.

∼

5

JACK

REMINDERS COME IN MANY FORMS.

I switched back and forth between staring out the window and watching her sleep. From where I sat, it didn't look like a peaceful sleep although, given the amount of vodka she'd consumed, and what her blood alcohol level likely was, I didn't figure it could be. At one point, her head lulled to the side and landed on the gentleman seated next to her. This is why I hate coach. I reached over and repositioned her head, offering a silent apology to the man by way of a glance.

"Where are you headed?" He spoke up minutes later after I'd turned my attention out the airplane window and onto the clouds below.

"Boston." I replied, but I didn't turn to face him when I answered. I wasn't in the mood for conversation.

"I gathered that much."

Amelie stirred.

"You two have family there?" he pried, clearly unable to take a hint.

Intending to get my point across, I shifted in his direction but somehow, when I saw the look on his face, I just couldn't do it. His eyes were tired. Maybe even sad. He had a certain look about him, his expression one of weariness. But I saw something else, too. Hope, perhaps. I shook my head. "No. A friend."

He nodded and I watched him visibly relax.

I motioned toward Amelie. "Or rather she has a friend."

He seemed to ponder what to say next—if anything at all. Finally, he spoke but kept it short and sweet. Which was exactly the way I like it.

"I see," he murmured and I thought we were done. I shifted once again and resumed staring out the window into the expanse.

However, to my dismay, he didn't stop there. How could I forget? They never do. "So, where is it you're staying in Boston?"

"I'm not sure," I replied meeting his eye once more. This time, I studied him more intently. His face seemed somehow softer and older than when I'd first glanced over. His hair was mostly gray, but if I looked hard enough, I could still make out a few strands of black. He had large brown eyes, the kind that seemed to see right through you. If you let them. "This one's trouble, no?" he remarked motioning toward a now drooling Amelie.

I nodded slightly. "Always has been. Probably always will be."

He smiled widely. "Those are the best kind, you know."

"Oh yeah? How's that?" I asked, cocking my head to one side.

"They're fighters. They know how to hang in there when the going gets tough."

"Yeah—well, neither one of us has ever been very good at the hanging around part."

He pursed his lips. "You've got time. You're still young…"

I chuckled. "That, I guess, is assuming either of us wants to hang around."

He coughed a bit and leaned forward. "You'll change your mind." He tried to assure me once he'd regained composure.

"Interestingly enough, it's never been my mind I was worried about changing." I paused and exhaled before continuing. "And quite honestly, I think the fighting part is sort of overrated."

"Not if you're dying, it isn't."

I swallowed. Hard. What the hell? That was it. I officially was done with the conversation.

"My wife is dying."

Or so I thought. What in the hell was I supposed to say to that? Nothing certainly didn't seem like an appropriate response. "Yeah, well, we all are," I quickly replied.

The man smiled, but it didn't touch his eyes. "Our son and his wife are having their first baby... the day after tomorrow. Apparently, these days, you kids schedule these things... it'll be our first grandchild. But—my wife, she's too sick to make the trip—and with airplanes being full of germs and all...well, she just couldn't be here. But that sure didn't stop her from demanding I come." I watched his mouth form a hard line. He laid his hands in his lap and shrugged. "So here I am," he said raising his hands in the air, and then folding them to rest in his lap once again. "But you know what? The only place I really want to be right now is by her side."

I looked over at Amelie briefly and then down at my shoes. "I can understand that."

Neither of us spoke again for some time afterward. The silence between us hung in the air like the last leaf hanging on in the fall. It was inevitable that with the right gust of wind, it would come down. It was just a matter of time.

Amelie stirred, smacking her lips together. She woke

slowly, rubbing at her eyes, and then all at once, she bolted upright and placed her hand on the man's forearm. "I'm sorry your wife couldn't be here, she offered hoarsely. I was taken aback. How did she fake sleep so well? And more importantly, how did she always know the simplest most right thing to say?

The man smiled. "Me too."

Amelie's gaze drifted over to me. I studied her expression. Her face now completely refreshed as though she'd just slept it all away, her demeanor youthful again, and she appeared lighter than she had been before her pretend nap. I watched as she picked up my bottle of water and took a sip.

She gulped half of the bottle down before turning her attention back to the man. "And I heard you say you were going to be a Grandpa."

The man beamed. "I am. They tell us it's a little boy..." He frowned slightly and looked at Amelie over to me and then back at her. "Everything's so different these days, though. We never knew half of the things you kids know today. It's almost as though nothing can be a surprise anymore."

"Isn't it amazing?" Amelie exclaimed. One small, at least half-fake nap and suddenly, she was a different person. This version of Amelie was on top of the world—full of energy and happy. So happy. The old man was wrong. Lots of things could surprise you. He just needed to hang around Amelie a little more.

"You should tell your wife to write the baby letters," she remarked, looking over at me. "That's what Jack's mom did when she got sick…"

I looked away and refocused my attention out the small window. I watched the clouds gather and form and then drift away. At that moment, I wanted to be one of them. Why was she bringing this up now? I hadn't thought about those letters in years.

"Hmmm. That sounds like a really good idea..." the man murmured.

"Oh, it is! Jack let me read a few of them and I tell you what—" she lowered her voice a few dozen octaves. "They really made an impact on me."

"I'm not sure though...her hands shake a lot these days." The man conceded. "I think it's the medication."

Amelie exhaled loudly. "Just give her a pen and see what happens. You might be surprised by the outcome if you hand her a renewed sense of purpose."

"You're a very wise young lady."

"My dad was a poet," Amelie mentioned cheerfully, and I could feel her eyes on me.

"That makes sense," the man replied.

I looked over at her then. She caught my gaze and didn't take her eyes off mine.

"I've actually started writing a bit here and there, too. But mostly—I take pictures."

"What do you photograph?"

Amelie's eyes bore into mine, and suddenly, I felt at ease. "All the beautiful things," she said.

"Of which there is no shortage," I added seconds later.

The man looked away. So did Amelie, focusing her attention ahead.

"Hey!" she eventually piped up, startling us both. The man looked over at her furtively. "I could take a photo or two of you and the baby—for your wife. You know, to make the trip a little more worth your while..."

The man considered her proposition before tearing up just slightly. Eventually, a small smile played across his lips. "You already have, my dear. You already have."

$\sim$

I drummed my fingers on my leg. Amelie had run off to the lavatory eighteen minutes ago and hadn't returned. I could hear her somewhere near the rear of the plane talking animatedly although I couldn't quite make out what she was saying.

The man looked my way and smiled. "Seems like she made another friend…"

I raised my brow. "That's Amelie for you."

He chuckled. "I gathered that."

"Well, it's a part of her anyway," I told him as I willed Amelie to get her ass back to her seat.

"I don't like to pry, son—but may I ask you a question?"

"Shoot," I said, although I didn't look directly at him.

"The letters your mother wrote…did they help?"

I sighed as I considered his question. "Not really," I told him as I shifted to fully face him. "Well, maybe," I relented, changing my mind. "I don't know. I haven't read them all…"

He nodded slowly and stretched his neck from side to side. "It's just that—I was thinking about my own son, that's all. He would never admit it, he's like his mother in that sense —but I can tell, apart from everything going on in his life, with his mother being sick and all—I can tell it's really tearing him up. That's hard for a father, you know."

I didn't know. But I improvised. "If you want the truth—I haven't read or thought about those letters in a very long time."

He appeared confused. "Why not?"

I answered without thinking too much about it. "My mother wasn't a fighter like your wife."

"Sure she was. She left you those letters, didn't she? In my opinion, there's a lot of defiance in that."

I picked at an invisible piece of lint on my pants. "I guess I never really looked at it that way."

"You know, son, none of us really knows what it's like to

be sick—until we are. I watch my wife suffer, and I want her to fight this—I really do. But in turn, it's hard to say what I would do if it were me laying there in that bed day in and day out. It's not easy watching her live out the remainder of her life—however long that may be in such a rotten way. So I can't imagine that it's any less hard being the one going through it all. She's either sick—or hurting—or missing something. Sometimes, even I—as much as I want her here, wonder if that's really living."

"I hear you." I agreed with a nod. "It's tough."

"Some fights take multiple rounds to win, you know. You don't always get it right straight out of the gate. "

I gathered that we were no longer just talking about my mother or his wife. "No, I guess you don't," I said, even though I didn't really believe what he was saying.

But the old man didn't stop there. It seemed he had something to say and he was determined to say it. "Look, all I know is this—if you love someone—you tell them. Work out the details later. The details... they're always variable anyhow. Take the weather, for example. We're really shitty at predicting it. That's what love is like...this is what I tell my kids—I tell them life and love are like a hurricane. You may think you have it all figured out. And then it washes ashore and you never know how terrible it's going to be—or not—until you're in the eye of the storm. But you can't stop a hurricane. You can only ride it out and then try to make sense of it all, once things are calm again. And they will be beautiful again as soon as the storm has passed. They'll likely be even better. Stronger. You'll be more prepared the next go 'round. And make no mistake there'll be another. There always is."

"Or—you can flee." I smirked. "I would argue that's the smartest plan."

The man shrugged. "Yes, but the storm comes all the

35

same. The question is where you wanna be and with whom you want to spend your time with when it hits."

6

AMELIE

'THE PURITAN CITY' TURNED OUT TO BE ANYTHING BUT.

*S*ome conversations you let happen. Others you force. Like with Jack and the old man, for instance. Jack was a mess. He wasn't going to admit it, of course, because, well—that's Jack.

But I knew it from the moment I saw him. Hidden behind that tall, dark, and handsome facade was a man who was tapped out. He likes to think I can't see right through him— but I can. Jack needs me right now every bit as much as I need him. If not more. And I'm not one of those women who need to be needed either. In fact, I abhor feeling needed. It makes me feel clammy and nauseous—and most importantly —it makes me want to run. But I'll deal with that later. For now, I'm happy. In fact, I'm over the moon.

"I've never cared for Boston," Jack remarked as we stepped out of the airport and into the night. The cold air hit hard, the bitter wind whipping my hair into my face. Of course, I'd forgotten to pack a coat. As though he read my mind, Jack shoved his suit jacket my way and demanded that I put it on. For one reason or another, he was in one of his odd moods yet again. Just as soon as we stepped off of that plane, all of a sudden, he turned pushy—all take and no give. Except for the jacket that is. Which I took, because it was cold and because he offered, and there's no sense in being cold, just to prove a point. I slipped it on and I thanked him, but after that, I did my best to ignore him, which worked for the entirety of the three minutes and forty-five seconds it took us to hail a cab.

He gave the cabbie the address and then turned to me. "You're sure you've told what's-his-name I'm coming with you?"

"It's Ian, Jack. His name is Ian."

"Right," he said as I watched his hands rub at his chin, and for the briefest of moments, I wanted to reach over and touch his face, too. "What kind of man doesn't take issue with his girlfriend bringing another man home for Thanksgiving?" And just like that, any inkling I had of putting my hands anywhere other than around his neck was instantly cured.

I rolled my eyes. "A secure man, that's what kind."

"Well, I'm a secure man. And I'd be finding myself a new girlfriend if I were in what's-his-name's shoes."

I threw up my hands. "IAN. His name is IAN!"

He mouthed Ian's name as he rolled his eyes, silently mocking me.

I let out a loud sigh, hesitated for a second, and then told the truth. "Also, I told him you were gay."

His eyes grew large and his jaw twitched. Still, I could tell that it hit him out of left field. "You are fucking kidding me."

I cocked my head and offered my best 'what do you think' face.

Jack shook his head and then shifted his body further away from mine. He didn't say anything for a long while. So I took out my phone and shot off a few emails. Eventually, when I looked over at him, I saw a small grin playing across his face. He noticed me looking and cleared his throat. I watched the grin fade as he looked over and nudged my arm, harder than I'd expected. "Guess what's-his-name isn't that secure after all, is he?"

I hit him. "Fuck you, Jack."

He laughed. "It'd probably make you happier, that's for sure."

As we made our way through the lobby of the crowded hotel, it struck me that I'd forgotten how beautiful this time of year was in Boston. The holiday decorations had already gone up and everyone seemed to be milling about humming as though in a trance-like state, glowing with the expectation of all that was yet to come. I could feel the buzz in the air, and it was the kind of thing that gave me goose bumps. The whole world seemed happy, and suddenly, knowing it made me perhaps the happiest of them all. Something shifted for me on that airplane and it had all started with a dream. I'd dreamt of my father—something I hadn't done in a very long time.

Jack seemed happier now, too. At check-in, he requested a separate room—a move for which I was grateful. Until, of course, we were informed that the hotel was full, and I realized we would be forced to share. A detail in which Jack didn't seem nearly as surprised or irritated about as I was. "It's not like we haven't done it before." He offered with a shrug.

"That's the problem," I said my mouth forming a hard line.

I adjusted my bag in my hand and shifted my weight from foot to foot. "Let's go up and get settled," I finally relented as I ushered him in my direction. For good measure, just so he didn't get the wrong idea, I added, "Then I'll text Ian and let him know we've arrived. I'm sure he'll want to meet us for a drink." I had only barely finished the sentence when my phone rang. Jack stopped in his tracks, looked down at the phone in my hand, and then up at me. He didn't have to say anything. His expression gave him away. He gently placed his hand on mine as he spoke. A peace offering. "Say you're tired. Tell him you'll see him tomorrow."

The ringing only seemed to grow louder. "I—I can't do that, Jack. He's expecting to see me."

He removed his hand, looked at the phone once more and shrugged. Then he turned and walked away. I pressed the button, silencing my phone and caught up with him at the elevator doors. Once inside, I watched as he deftly pressed the number for the fourteenth floor and then ran his fingers through his hair. "Why are you staying in this hotel anyway?" He frowned. "It's not your style..."

I watched his reflection in the mirrored walls. "What do you mean?"

"I mean who booked the room?"

I furrowed my brow. "Ian did. Why?"

He nodded and the shook his head slightly. "No reason. I was just curious."

I watched the numbers light up as the elevator rose and wondered why he had to be such an ass. But as we stepped out of the elevator, I did my best to let it go. He'd made the trip to Boston for me, and the least I could do was cut him some slack.

Jack found our room as I fumbled around in search of the room key. Exasperated, I looked up only to find him dangling it in front of me. "I don't know what you'd do without me," he chided.

I grabbed the key card from his hand and slid it into the slot in the door. How I do it without him. Seriously? My patience was running thin. "Somehow I manage," I assured him, stepping inside. Jack followed.

Immediately, I slung my bags to the floor and plopped down on the bed closest to the windows and text Ian.

Jet-lagged. Super tired. Going to bed. Call you in the morning. Early. Love you.

Seconds later, I received a response.

Really? Are you sure? I've been waiting up... I miss you. Ian.

I chewed on my bottom lip as I rattled off a response. Short and sweet, just the way he liked it:

I'm sure. I've missed you too. Can't wait to see you. But must sleep now. I'd be lousy company anyhow. Call you mañana. XO

All right then. Rest up. Can't wait to see you. We have a big week ahead of us. Sweet dreams. I love you. Ian

I read his text, clicked my phone off, and tossed it onto the bed. Then I turned to Jack, who'd clearly been watching me. He raised his brow. "Everything ok?"

I smiled and then crawled to the edge of the bed. "Let's do something crazy!"

"I thought you were 'going to bed'?"

I offered up the most serious go-to-hell look I could muster. "Why would you say that?"

"Just an educated guess."

I hopped off the bed, put my hands on my hips and waited. "Well?

Jack sighed. "Can I shower first?"

"Have at it," I said, I motioning toward the bathroom.

I watched as he strode across the room like he'd just won the lottery. Jack always had liked winning. It was the fact that he couldn't stop playing the game that was the issue. Jack's problem was that he'd never learned how to count his blessings, quit while he was ahead, and call it a day. And because I knew Jack, I knew he probably never would.

He closed the bathroom door only to open it again a few seconds later. Shirtless, of course. "Hey, kid?" he called.

"No, Jack," I told him even though I wanted to say yes. Yes, I'll shower with you. I wanted to say yes. But thankfully, at least one of us knew how to quit while we were ahead.

He looked genuinely confused. "No? What?"

I shook my head. "Never mind."

"I was just going to say...for what it's worth—that if it were me—I would have put you up in a better hotel. One with history... the kind you like."

I didn't respond. At least not with words. Because even if I'd had the right ones, I wouldn't have been able to force the lump that had formed in my throat out of the way.

～

7

JACK

WE REALLY MESSED UP.

*S*he said she wanted to do something crazy. Which pretty much turned out to be code for 'let's fuck everything up.' It always had. And for the most part, I played right into it.

'Operation let's fuck everything up' first began when we arrived at a little hole in the wall, dive bar, where Amelie insisted that I take a shot with her. "Just one." She pleaded all doe-eyed, innocently beckoning my demise.

Did I mention that I hate bars? Well, this place, I'm pretty sure is the worst of them all. It was dank and musty and dimly lit. Not to mention, crowded and loud—all of the things I abhor. Out of all the nicer more upscale places we could've chosen along the way, she picked this one. Only God knows why.

"I heard the music was good here." Amelie leaned in close to say as though she'd read my mind. "Come on, one shot— maybe two for me and then we'll go…" She begged as she yanked on my hand.

"What are we, twenty-two again?

"Twenty-two, thirty-two? Who cares! Let's have fun, Jacky!'"

I hate it when she calls me that. And she knows it too, which is why she only does it after she's had one too many. "Jack." I correct her. "And you may be thirty-two, but I'm not."

"Oh yeah… you're soooo old." She told me slurring her words as she spoke, having already cleaned out the mini-bar back at the hotel.

I watched as she ordered two shots. When the bartender placed them on the bar, she picked one up and shoved it in my direction. I tilted my head and considered her for a moment. "You know I don't drink."

She waved me off. "You always say that! But I've seen you have one or two here and there. So—you can't exactly call yourself a teetotal," she told me as she clinked my glass with hers and eyed me expectantly. She looked so enthusiastic that I thought 'ah, what the hell' and I slammed the shot back. I didn't use a chaser and neither did she. I didn't drink it solely because she insists. There were eyes on us and I sensed them watching curiously. And while I had never been one to conform or to cave to the pressure of the crowd, I drank it because I knew one drink wouldn't kill me. Still, there was the fact Amelie had always had this way of making me do what she wanted. It was what I both loved and hated about her.

It turned out, however, that my assumption about one not killing me turned out to be almost wrong. One led to another as it usually does. Three shots in, and not only do I probably look like a lightweight, but I also felt like one, too. It hit me then that I hadn't eaten dinner, and when you combine a lack of adequate food consumption with not being a drinker to begin with, the combination equals an easy drunk.

Amelie watched me for a moment and then she shimmied

up close and whispered in my ear. "Let go, Jack. Just let go a little." And her voice was so smooth and she smelled so good that I forgot there was ever any other choice.

IT WAS COLD OUT AND ALL I COULD THINK ABOUT WAS GOING back to the hotel because if there was anything I didn't like, it was the feeling I had lost control. My head was swimming, my stomach churning and yet we'd just arrived at our second bar of the night where, once again, Amelie had demanded we order drinks. I told her I was good. By this point, I was certain I'd said this a few times. But it didn't stop her. She left me standing there and then returned holding two beers, wearing a huge grin on her face. This bar was different from the last place—it was a little more modern, only with crappier music and more expensive, over-priced drinks.

As I was considering my exit strategy, she took my hand, and I realized I'd forgotten how well we fit together. All of a sudden, I looked up and she was leading me to the edge of the dance floor. I studied her profile as she propped herself against a metal beam and eyed the crowd. I think some old Madonna song was playing, but I couldn't be sure because whatever it was, it wasn't my taste. She watched the people and I watched her. She had on skinny jeans, thigh-high high-heeled boots, and a tiny little sweater that showed her midriff whenever she raised her arms. Looking at her standing there like that made me think of other women I had dated—but mostly it just made me want to do very bad things to her. Then I remembered it was Amelie—not one of those other women, and suddenly, I longed to lean in and kiss her. But I didn't. I knew she wasn't ready for more, and aside from that, she'd very clearly had too much to drink. It wasn't my style.

I stared at her lower back and was considering the way it ever so slightly touched the beam when she turned, caught my eye, and leaned forward. "I wanna dance, Jack. I think we should dance!" she screamed in my ear, even though there wasn't reason to.

"I don't," I said, shaking my head and her gaze burned into mine.

Seconds later, she shoved her beer into my chest. Already, I knew where this was going—and I didn't like it. "Fine. Hold this," she demanded and I watched as she skipped out onto the dance floor.

She wasn't out there for more than thirty seconds or so when the music changed to some crap hip-hop stuff, and true to form, Amelie went all in. I studied the way she moved her body as though no one was watching—when so many people obviously were. As I watched, I found her moves amusing even though I was perturbed that she'd just left me standing there holding her drink. She doesn't look my way even though I know she knows I'm watching.

Unfortunately, however, for the both of us, I wasn't the only one. I watched as two former frat boys sidled up to her, and I knew instantly what was about to go down. Immediately, they got too close for my liking and Amelie moved away. Apparently, they didn't take the hint. Boys like them never do. And all of a sudden—I didn't know if it was the alcohol—or my irritation over the fact that a girl can't even enjoy a dance without two assholes manhandling her—but in two strides I was on the floor. Maybe I said something threatening, maybe I didn't. I don't even remember, honestly. But the next thing I know people were being shoved. There's a scuffle, and suddenly, I was being led out of the club by two former semi-pro wrestler looking guys, and I was reminded once again why I hate shit-hole places like this.

"Well, you didn't have to go and get us kicked out, Jack,"

Amelie said dramatically when she found me waiting outside by the curb. "I just wanted to dance!"

"That's the problem," I told her, no longer in the mood to deal with her drunkenness. It's funny how quickly one could sober up at the prospect of having to defend yourself against former frat boys double-teaming you. "You know I hate places like this."

She moves in closer. "Then why'd you come?" she shouted for no good reason. I was well within earshot.

"To protect you from exactly the kind of thing that just happened," I shot back louder than I'd intended. By this point, we had onlookers.

"Did it ever occur to you that I'm just fine on my own?"

"You don't look just fine. You look drunk."

"And you look like an asshole."

"Haven't we had this conversation before?" I asked. "Because this certainly feels like déjà vu to me."

She shook her head, threw her hands up, and stormed off in the opposite direction. "I thought you were my friend," she called back over her shoulder. "Now you're just being mean." Her face fell. "I'm not sure we should be friends anymore," she told me, most of her rationale gone by way of her soberness.

I don't respond because this is drunk Amelie talking. She always reverted back to that eight-year-old girl I remember from camp whenever she drinks. I smiled even though I wanted to kill her. And I follow, of course.

Yet I stood back just a little as she tried with no luck to hail a cab.

After witnessing several painful attempts, I showed off my whistling skills and helped her out—even though what I really wanted was for her to have to work for it. Only, it was cold out and there was no point in being cold just to prove a point.

She shot me a defiant look as I held the door of the cab open for her. It's her best attempt to convey that she would have been fine on her own. But she wouldn't have.

"I need food," she said looking out the window and her voice sounded about as childish as she'd been acting.

Once I'd instructed the cabbie to take us to a decent diner, I patted her knee and told her we would get her all fixed up. It's a statement, which only seems to irritate her further, and so I leave it at that.

Thirty minutes later, we were seated across from each other in annoyed silence. She ordered enough food to feed the both of us and maybe a few others. Finally, it was me who broke the ice. "I thought you weren't supposed to be drinking with your medication." I mumble the words, and I know it's only going to piss her off—yet I can't help myself.

She paused mid-bite and then looked up. "I don't take medication."

"What do you mean?" I asked even though it's pretty clear what she meant.

She shrugged. "I just decided to stop taking it one day several years back. And I've been fine." She took a sip of her water and swallowed. "Better than fine."

I tread carefully, but not too carefully. "You don't seem fine."

"Well, I am," she told me and she let me know she was serious by the way her eyes bugged out as she said it.

The waitress came to check on us then and Amelie ordered pie even though she'd eaten most of the food she had ordered. She really didn't need it. I was afraid she was going to be sick. But I didn't say so. "When's the last time you ate?"

She wasn't thrilled with my finesse. "Why do you ask so many questions?"

I smiled. "I'm a curious person."

Amelie shook her head and then rolled her eyes. "I don't know...maybe lunchtime yesterday."

I nod even though I'd figured as much, and then I eye the few remnants of her triple pancake, triple egg, and bacon meal. "Well, it's a good thing you ordered the pie because, personally, I think you need to eat a little more. You can't possibly be full."

She followed my gaze and we both smiled. She knew I was full of shit, but also that I knew her better than she'd like to believe.

And just like that, we're friends again.

BACK AT THE HOTEL, I SHOWERED ONCE AGAIN WHILE AMELIE climbed straight into bed. By the time I came out, she was fast asleep, sprawled out fully clothed. She wasn't sick as I figured she would be given the amount of alcohol and food she had consumed and this worried me. She must do this kind of thing more often than I'd hoped. I wanted to wake her, but I didn't. I unzipped her boots, slipped them off, and pulled the duvet back. I wanted to slip her out of her clothes, but I didn't. I simply arranged the covers, pulled them up, and turned off the light. Then I climbed into the opposite bed. Only I didn't sleep. I listened to her inhale and then exhale, and I counted the time between her breaths for several minutes. Then I dimmed the screen on my phone, just in case, even though I knew she was out cold. I did a little work. At some point, I dozed off because the next thing I knew, Amelie was crawling in bed next to me. Half asleep, I scooted over to make room even though I knew it was a bad idea.

"I had a bad dream," she told me and her breath reeked of syrup and alcohol.

"I'm not sleeping with you, Amelie."

She lifted her head, and I could tell by her tone that she had sobered up some. "That's very presumptuous of you," she told me, her voice low.

"I don't sleep with drunk women."

She sighed and then cuddled up next to me. She reached for my arm and placed it just below her rib cage. I felt the warmth of her body and I wanted to fuck her, I really did. But luckily, I have major self-restraint. I knew when to play my cards and when to hold 'em.

"Jack?" she whispered.

"Hm?"

"Aren't you, though? Technically...sleeping with a drunken woman?" she remarked as she pushed her finger into my chest.

I smile and I pulled her in a little closer.

"No," I said. "I'm wide awake."

WITH THE MORNING LIGHT CAME CLARITY AND SOBERNESS, AND there we were—tangled up in each other. I opened my eyes and checked the time on the clock opposite the bed. 7:30 AM. She said she would call him early. Not that I cared. What I did care about, however, was her keeping her word. So I shook her gently until she stirred. When she didn't immediately open her eyes, I nudged her again. "What time are we supposed to meet what's-his-name?" Admittedly, I liked the way 'we' sounded.

She opened her eyes then and squinted to see the clock. Her face twisted, and she went from waking up slowly to waking all at once. Then, the next thing I knew, her mouth was on mine. I pulled away slightly. This isn't like her. No, wait…this is exactly like her. "We need to get this over with," she said, breathless.

"That's very presumptuous of you," I replied, appearing confused even though I wasn't.

"So what." She grinned and then added a slight shrug for good measure. Next, she was climbing on top of me and tugging my shirt over my head. You know how people say, 'it just happened.' Well, this was sort of like that. Only it didn't just happen. We'd both—clearly or not so clearly—made the decision that it was what we wanted, although neither of us wanted to discuss it. All of a sudden, I was kissing her from head to toe, and I was slipping off her clothes, and then she was pulling me inside of her, and oh, fuck, this was really happening.

And, happen, it did. But it was rushed sex. The kind that's full of passion, sloppy, and still decent—but not as good as it could've been had we taken our time. I'd wanted to take my time, but a part of me was afraid she'd change her mind. And for that, I knew I'd hate myself a little in the end.

I realize I probably shouldn't have had sex with her. But this time she was sober. Also, I'm a guy, not an idiot, and when you're a guy and there's a beautiful woman in your bed offering herself up to you, you don't say no. That's just not the way guys work—even those of us with self-control.

Women, on the other hand, act with their emotions. They go through with things if they feel the moment is right and regret it later. Men, we almost never regret sex. We regret other things. But rarely the sex.

Amelie dug her nails into my back as I finished, just shortly after she had, and we both lay there, out of breath, neither of us willing to break the silence.

Although, this time, it would be Amelie who spoke first. Just as it should have been. After all, she's the one who started this. I simply finished it. "You know, Jack…" she said, her voice surprisingly playful, "that really wasn't your best."

I turned to face her. She grinned and I took her chin in my hand. "Then I guess we'll just have to do it again…" I said, partly testing her.

She understood it was more of a question than a statement.

"We'll see," she answered in a non-committal tone. Then she smiled.

Only that smile was quickly wiped right off her face by a knock at the door. She bolted straight up, covering herself, her face losing all of its color.

"It's just housekeeping," I tried to assure her.

Her eyes trailed to the clock. There was another knock. She jumped out of bed and looked at me. Her eyes grew wider. "Shit, I think it's Ian," she whispered through gritted teeth.

"I got that," I said as I stood and pulled on my pajama pants.

"Oh, my God," she cried, her hand flying to her mouth.

I took her by the shoulders. "Go get in the shower. I've got this."

She considered what I was proposing for a second, connecting the dots. Finally, she nodded. And then she turned, walked to the bathroom and closed the door. I picked my t-shirt up, slid it over my head, giving her enough time to run the shower before I went to the door and opened it.

Standing there before me was none other than one pissed off looking man. "I've been calling all morning," he said hurriedly, which seemed to be all he could get out. And that's what he led with.

I ran my fingers through my hair and tried out my best sleepy, gay voice. "I'm sorry, brother," I told him sleepily as I rubbed at my eyes. "I just woke up."

His anger dissipated but only a little. I could tell he wasn't sold so I stepped aside and ushered him inside. "I got in late," I added with a decent fake yawn. "Turns out Boston's a playground for boys like me."

He eyed me up and down, looking quite perplexed and unsure of what to say. "Jack," I said, extending my hand as flamboyantly as I could muster.

"Ian." He nodded. But he didn't shake my hand.

The trouble was this could only mean one of two things. Either he bought my story. Or he didn't.

❧

8

AMELIE

BEING BACKED AGAINST THE WALL ONLY GETS YOU SCREWED...

I honestly didn't know what to make of my current situation. I was in a low mood. That's about as much as I knew. Very, very low. But I was hiding it well. That was the good news.

The bad news was sleeping with Jack. It was a mistake—a gigantic fucking mistake of epic proportions. That's the best way I can think to describe it. And the worst part was I didn't even have the drinking or being hungover to blame. There was nothing but my poor decision-making to blame. The truth was, these days I don't even get hungover anymore. They say that can be a sign of alcoholism. But I'm not an alcoholic. I know this because I took one of those 'am I an alcoholic tests' you can find online, and sure enough, it confirmed what I already knew—that I'm just a girl who likes to have fun. Which is exactly what I thought I was doing with Jack Harrison—until I realized what I was actually doing was giving him an in.

To add to the bitter taste of regret, there was also the fact that Ian was acting incredibly strange. Then again, Ian always acted strange. But this time, I was worried. It's been exactly sixty-seven days—if my count was correct—since he had slept with the twenty-year-old intern down in marketing. I know this because Ian is the sort of guy who marks his affairs on his calendar. And every so often, I like to take a peek—just to ensure that I'm not wrong.

Although I use the term 'affair' loosely because, the truth is—I don't care. It doesn't bother me in the least that he sleeps around on occasion. I know that sounds bad—made even worse by the fact that he thinks we're exclusive when he's so obviously getting his on the side. As for me, I've very carefully dabbled here and there—but just once or twice. For the most part, I simply pour myself into my work. I don't really care what Ian does with the girl from marketing or the other one who lives in his building down the hall—because the truth of the matter is, I don't see much of a future with Ian. Why I'm still with him, when I know this, well—that is a very good question. One with a very complex answer. The answer being something I've thought about over and over during my darker days. For one, there's the fact that as long as I am 'with him,' I don't have to be with anyone else. Ian is a safety net. He's a safe bet, and with him, I know exactly what I'm getting. Each and every time, I might add.

Mainly, though, there's the issue of the 'the very bad thing.' This is what Ian likes to remind me of when I pull away. This is also another reason—one of many, I don't care about the girl in marketing. Not really, anyway. That girl does me a favor, truthfully. She gives me an out. Or rather—Ian gives me an out.

He knows I know and this buys me space and the right to be indifferent toward him. It's the one reason I'm 'allowed' to be angry. Sleeping around, or the other women I should say gives him the validation he needs to believe that I actually do care about him. It's a twisted game we play. I know this.

Still, there's the issue of 'the very bad thing.' 'The very bad thing,' as Ian likes to call it, is something I did in South America about two months after Jack left me asleep, without warning. The truth is I was kind of a mess after that. I'd sunk to a low of which depths I hadn't known before. Both creatively and personally, I was a wreck. This was all pre-Ian. I wasn't getting the shots I needed—and yet the trip had already been extended by sixty days, and I was quickly running out of time. If I turned up empty handed, I knew my job was on the chopping block. That's the thing about being a photographer. There's always someone with more gumption and drive willing to take your job for less pay in a heartbeat. I knew this and yet it only contributed to the unending list of excuses I had for not getting out of bed. Until, day-by-day, the self-loathing became worse and worse until I'd pretty much run out of options. And in that kind of low, I couldn't seem to talk myself out of the nagging feeling that I'd already lost a dear friend and lover. Next up was the only thing I really had left—my career—and what did it all really matter anyhow.

Eventually, out of options and out of time, I made a split-second decision that would seal my fate for years to come—if not forever. This was when I did the 'very bad thing.' Ironically enough, it was so easy to put into motion, yet impossible to stop once I'd gone through with it.

One day, I was out in the market, attempting to photograph the locals. This hadn't been why I'd come to South America nor was it really what I should have been spending my time shooting. A chance encounter month's prior led me to meet the girl that would forever alter the course of my life. Perhaps the saddest part of it all was that I couldn't even remember what her name was. I like to pretend it was Isabel —although I can't be sure. 'Isabel' was a local photographer who I'd interacted with on several occasions during my time there. The moment I saw her, standing there in the market, I knew. I'd ask her advice on the shots I needed. In the end, I hired her to take them. The 'very bad' part was that I'd submitted them to the magazine as my own. 'Isabel' was a Venezuelan girl who was just happy to have the eight hundred bucks I paid her. She took the most amazing photos and had no qualms about how, or why, she was doing so. Everything would have been fine if my assistant at the time hadn't known about the entire thing.

Two months after the photos went to publication said assistant went to my boss. I'll probably never know why she did it—other than the fact that she wanted my job, but it was what it was.

In the end, however, I wound up mostly unscathed, with a slap on the wrist. It turned out to be a very lucky break—nothing more than undeserved grace, really. Also, that assistant was promoted and transferred, and now I have Erica. It was win-win, thankfully. And so, the very bad thing pretty much stopped there.

That was until Ian came on the scene. We'd been sleeping together for about six weeks when he brought it up out of the blue one night after we'd just had sex. I'd gone all out in my performance—so much so that I was still a bit shaky while he wore the afterglow of time well spent. That's when the shoe dropped, so to speak.

He'd suggested that we make a pot of coffee and go over the photographs I'd taken which I had not so secretly been hoping he would feature in the upcoming issue. The photographs were the premise of why he had called me over to his place at ten p.m. on a Tuesday. Even though that wasn't actually why at all.

As he stirred his coffee, I watched him study my work, and I could tell while he wasn't in love with them, I knew he was in love with me. Although the joke turned out to be on me. At the time, I hadn't yet learned the whole truth about the kind of man Ian was and his unique ability to draw lines where he thought they ought to be drawn.

"So you think you'll include them, then?" I asked, hopeful. I remember the way he looked up at me quizzically. I thought I saw fondness in his expression and then all at once, I saw it fade.

He inhaled slowly and let it out. "You know, I'm not sure. These photos…" I watched him pick them up one by one and then shove them aside. "They remind me of the ones you took in Venezuela to be frank."

I cocked my head. He continued. "And I'm not sure that's the style we're going for here."

"I'm not sure what you mean," I replied, caught completely off guard.

"This just doesn't look like your work, that's all."

"It is my work."

He stood and walked over to the coffee pot. "But how can I be sure?" he remarked, adding to his mug, yet not taking his eyes off mine.

"Because I'm telling you they are," I said my voice coming out more high pitched than I'd hoped.

"Amelie… my darling… if there's one thing you must know about me, it's that I don't simply trust people because they tell me I should. And now that I'm running things in our department—well, things are going to be a little different around the magazine. So, if you want your work featured— you're going to have to work for it just like anyone else." He took a sip of coffee and then blew on his cup. "I don't play favorites, my dear—" I watched him walk around the counter and back over to the table, stopping just in front of me. He pointed to the bedroom and then let his hand drop. "No matter what just happened in there."

"I never asked you to." I frowned.

He came closer and placed his hand on my shoulder. "I'm

a businessman, Amelie. You want something—then you're going to have to earn it. And I sure won't have a lying hack on my team." He squeezed my shoulder. "Do I make myself clear?"

I nodded, and then stood, scanning the living room for my clothes. "You're not going to rush off now, are you?" he asked watching me.

"I really need to get home," I called out, not slowing down.

Ian cornered me in his living room and took me by both shoulders, forcing me to look at him. "No," he said, his expression serious. "What you need is to come to bed."

"No. I—I think I'm gonna go...Clearly you have the wrong idea about me."

"Amelie. Oh, Amelie." He shook his head. "And here I was thinking that we had something here—that we could make this little thing between us work. I'm sad to see that you're trying to prove me wrong. A little criticism and you bail..."

I backed away. "I'm not bailing. I'm tired."

Ian locked his eyes on mine. "Tell me, do you value your job?"

"Of course, I do." I snapped.

"Well, then, you'll come to bed. You'll show me that a tad bit of criticism won't turn you off." He sighed, paused and let this voice linger. "If you want that promotion, then these are all things you're going to have to work on. Not just the quality of your work—but your ability to remain neutral."

By this point, I was gathering my clothes, trying to piece them together. "I'm feeling pretty neutral," I assured him.

"About Venezuela..." he chimed in, "you're lucky you have kept your job, you know? Plagiarism is a very serious offense. In fact, I was shocked when I heard. It just didn't seem like you." He waved his hands dramatically as he continued. "It was a little hiccup, I get it—but it's a hiccup that could cause you to never be able to land another job in this industry. I mean, if word were to get out..."

I threw on my blouse not even bothering to button it. "And why would it?"

"I don't know." He shrugged. "You know how people talk."

I stepped into my jeans, pulling them up as quickly as I could, still nearly tripping over myself. "And what would people say if they knew you were sleeping with a subordinate," I demanded.

"There aren't rules against that."

I grabbed my clutch from the entry table. "If you say so," I huffed as I turned away from him and started toward the door. "I'm going..." I called over my shoulder.

Suddenly, his hand gripped my wrist. "Sweetheart," he said his voice lower, "don't go. Not like this. I want to see you succeed. I do! But you can't think you can just waltz in here, fuck my brains out, and get what you want. I'm not that kind of man. I've known many girls like you, you see."

"Fuck you, Ian." I tried to pull away from his grip to no avail.

He leaned forward and attempted to kiss my cheek. "I know you're angry—but in time, you'll come to see that I was right."

"I doubt that."

He released my wrist and I opened the door.

"Well, if nothing else, you'll understand that I'm simply trying to make you better."

I shook my head, slammed the door, and didn't look back.

THE FOLLOWING DAY, I CONSULTED AN ATTORNEY ABOUT MY predicament. I wanted to see what my options were, and unfortunately, what I learned was pretty much what I'd assumed. There was nothing I could do if Ian fired me. According to HR, he was right in that he wasn't breaking any rules by sleeping with me. He was also likely correct, according to the attorney, that if I were fired for plagiarism, I would probably not be able to find gainful employment within the industry. Basically, the attorney informed me within ten short minutes, for the price of one hundred and eighty dollars, that I was in one hell of a pickle.

I returned back from my meeting with the attorney to find a dozen white roses sitting atop my desk with a note that read:

Don't do anything rash. This is me raising my white flag by way of flowers. This is me saying I'm sorry. Yours, Ian

I didn't care that he was sorry. I was done. I figured I might end up getting canned—but at least I'd have my dignity intact.

This rift between us lasted for twelve days until the office Christmas party interrupted my good intentions. I hated the holidays. Everyone was merry and I was alone. I don't remember ever feeling as utterly alone as I did that Christmas. I hadn't spoken to Jack in months, and I didn't figure that I would. I didn't have a family—other than my mom, who was in the Bahamas with her latest boyfriend for the holidays.

I had actually been mulling over what I might do for Christmas seeing that most of my friends had families of their own and those who didn't, had at least someone special enough to have made plans with them. As I reached for another glass of champagne from the server's tray, Ian intercepted. He told me he needed to speak with me, alone and led me by the hand to his office. But not before I'd downed the remainder of the champagne in my glass. I'd already consumed at least four of them prior. He handed me his half-empty glass as he closed the door. I watched as he locked it. "I can't see," I said, slurring a bit, still sober enough to realize I was doing so. His office was mostly dark, with all of the shades drawn.

"It's better this way," he purred. I took a sip of his drink even though I'd already had enough. The room was spinning just a little as I felt him come closer. "Hi there," he said and the next thing I knew he was running his hands up my rib cage. "Drink the champagne, Amelie. We have something to celebrate." He motioned, eying the glass. As I stepped backward, I found myself up against the wall, in more ways than one.

"Oh?" I asked. He grinned as he took a strand of my hair between his fingers.

"I'm going to publish your photos," he said, leaning in and whispering into my ear, his breath hot and minty. I tried to move away yet I couldn't make much headway. "But not because of this," he murmured, sliding his hand between my legs. I had to admit it felt so good that I almost wanted him to keep going. Instead, he stopped, pulled back, and looked directly at me. "Are you happy?" he asked. I considered his question. But my head was swimming and not much made any sense in that moment. I wanted him to touch me, I wanted him to tell me that he wanted me, too, and I hated myself for it.

"Yes. Very," I assured him, downing the champagne.

"You're lying. I've been watching you," he told me stepping forward as he pinned me once again. "I didn't hear you say thank you."

"Thank you," I managed to choke out. He slipped a finger into my panties. "Do you like it when I touch you?"

"Yes," I said, suddenly drunk on everything. Champagne,

the relief of not feeling so alone, the joy that he'd chosen my work, hope that I might not be fired after all...

"Do you know what you do to me?" he demanded, as he came up for air, his mouth sucking and biting on my neck.

I shook my head.

"For twelve days, I've watched you prance around here all melancholy-like, and you know what I've wanted to do? I wanted to fuck that melancholy right out of you. But I couldn't because I had to teach you a lesson. You don't toy with me, Amelie. I'm a man, yes, but I have feelings." He stopped kissing me and looked me square in the eye. "And I know when I'm being used."

I swallowed hard. "I'm not using you."

Ian leaned, kissed me hard, taking my bottom lip between his teeth. He bit down and then released it slowly. "Sure you are," he said, before he slipped one finger inside me, plunging deep, causing every fiber in my body to tense. "And now it's my turn."

He pulled out and then pushed his finger in deeper this time. "Do you like this?"

I nodded.

"Turn around. I want you to pull your dress over your hips and place your hands on the wall. I want to see you."

I did as I was told. I could feel his eyes on me. It felt like forever before he spoke again.

"Arch your back," he finally ordered.

I did as he asked as I placed my forehead against the coolness of the wall to steady myself.

"Are you drunk, Amelie?" he asked, grabbing my ass.

"No." I squirmed

"Don't lie to me," he said after making a clucking sound with his tongue. "I was sure you'd know better by now..."

"I'm not."

"Are you drunk?"

"Maybe a little," I relented

I felt him trail one finger along my backside. Then he pushed my panties to the side.

"Do you like feeling out of control."

"No!"

He smacked my ass hard. I flinched. It stung. "You're lying again."

"I'm not," I promised.

"Tell me you want me to use you."

"I can't."

"Why not?"

I sighed, drunkenly. "Because I don't."

"What do you want then, Amelie?"

"I don't know."

He slapped my other ass cheek. This hit hurt worse. "Sure you do."

I tried to swallow the sting away.

"Well…" he demanded, and I felt him rear his hand back once again.

"I want you to fuck me."

"That's what I thought," he said as he'd positioned himself behind me.

And fuck me, he did. Right there against his office wall.

It had been a long time since I'd been fucked like that.

Not since Jack.

"I'M NOT SURE I LIKE YOUR FRIEND," IAN EXCLAIMED OVER breakfast, interrupting my thoughts. "What are thinking about?" he asked eyeing the waitress. "You seem far off."

I smiled. "The office Christmas party."

"I see." He beamed.

Ian was hungry and had decided the three of us should

have breakfast at the hotel before getting on the road and driving the hour that it would take to get to his parents place. Thankfully, Jack had bowed out saying he was too hungover to eat and needed a shower anyhow.

I watched as Ian carefully cut his food. "Did you hear what I said?" He didn't wait for me to answer. "I don't think I like your friend…"

"I'm sorry to hear that," I replied between bites. "Because he's my oldest and dearest friend, Ian."

He picked at his Eggs Benedict. "I should be your dearest friend." He took a bite and chewed. "And I think he's in love with you."

I dropped my fork. "You are my dearest boyfriend. Also, I've told you a million times that Jack is gay."

The diners seated beside us stared. Ian either didn't notice or didn't care.

"Why did he even come? You just sprung this on me and my poor mother—and, well, neither of us were expecting an extra guest. And you know how I hate surprises."

I lowered my voice. "I told you—he didn't have anyone to spend Thanksgiving with."

"And?"

"And I wanted him to meet you."

"Yeah, well, I don't like you sharing a room with him. You didn't tell me you were sharing a room with him!" His face reddened as his voice grew louder.

I raised my voice as I spoke, not caring who was listening. "Ian, we've been together for almost a year and a half, I've just flown halfway around the country to spend Thanksgiving with your family when it was technically out of my way, and you're letting me know now that you don't trust me?"

He placed his hand on mine and softened, although not much. "It's not you I don't trust."

I looked up at him and smiled before turning serious. "Oh, Ian," I lamented. "Jack is harmless. I don't know how you can't see that." I raised my mimosa to my lips. "And besides, I really didn't come all this way to fight with you."

He considered me for a moment and then he exhaled. "You know... you're right—I'm sorry. I don't want to ruin Thanksgiving with my nonsense. If you tell me I can trust you, well, then, I'm going to trust you. I know you have too much riding on this relationship to go and mess it all up with someone like that anyway."

"Someone like what?" I couldn't help but ask. I knew I shouldn't have taken the bait and yet I stop myself.

"Someone there's no future with..."

"Ah," I remarked my mouth forming a hardline.

"And, in any case, if you two really had a thing for one another you most certainly would have already done something about it by now."

I laughed but just a little. "You're forgetting one thing," I told him.

"What's that?" he asked raising his brow.

"Jack is gay."

~

9

JACK

I HATE HER. I HATE HER NOT. I—

From the first moment I laid eyes on what's-his-name, I despised him. Instantly, I could tell what kind of guy Ian Larson was—a small-minded, egotistical, control freak.

What Amelie sees in him or why she's with him, I haven't a clue. In addition, I'm pretty sure that he hadn't bought the story that there was nothing between his girlfriend and I. And to be honest, if it hadn't been for Amelie, and if I hadn't slept with her that morning, I would have bailed the moment he showed up at the door. I don't have time for the kind of bullshit a guy like him presents. I'm shocked that Amelie does. It makes me wonder if I even know her at all.

But I did sleep with her—and so bailing would've made me look like an asshole. But my staying also wasn't purely unselfish. The truth was I wanted to sleep with her again. And again. But first, I figured I had to get through all the bullshit and red tape, better known as Ian Larson and his stupid fucking Thanksgiving plans.

So, I showered and met them down near the parking garage where we got into Ian's car and he drove us out to his parent's estate. The drive was awkward to say the least. Amelie barely spoke and when she did, she didn't meet my eye. I don't recall speaking much either. Ian did enough running his mouth for the both of us.

I could already tell on the drive in that the place, and likely its occupants were going to be pretentious pricks. Just like their son. And sure enough, I was right. They lived in a small suburb just outside of the city. Their home was a large Tudor style house that I wanted to dislike but couldn't. Luckily, I didn't have the same issue with Ian's parents. Mrs. Larson was slim, her smile fake, her face plastic, and her most favorite thing was perhaps a toss-up between name dropping and talking down to people. She excelled at both as though, aside from her appearance, these were her only two missions in life. As for Mr. Larson, he clearly had excelled at producing progeny that were exact replicas of himself.

Dinner was catered, of course, and there were about forty or so people in attendance. Most of them, I found to be just as dreadful as their hosts were. Only one stuck out as original and down to earth, and she was for the most part occupied. With Amelie tied up, I considered how to bow out gracefully. Only just as I began to make my escape, Mrs. Larson took me by the hand and announced that dinner was being served. So, I took one for the team and stuck around, against my better judgment but kept the number I'd Googled for car services handy, just in case.

By the time the second course was brought around, the conversation had become all but unbearable. It was a matter of minutes before I'd planned to excuse myself citing an emergency. I could tell Amelie was over it too, and I hoped that she'd bow out with me, despite the fact she was doing her best to put on a good show.

I was seated to the right of Amelie. Ian was seated to her left, and as the turkey was brought out, I nudged her to get her attention. As everyone oohed and ahhed over the bird, I felt Amelie squeeze my thigh under the table. She glanced over at me, and I realized it was the first time she'd really looked at me since that morning in bed. She smiled and I saw it for what it was—a silent apology. In her expression, I understood all the things she wanted to say. She wanted to tell me she was sorry for bringing me here, sorry we hadn't had more time, and most of all that she was sorry we'd spent so long apart. I nodded at her and then watched in slow motion as what's-his-name clicked his crystal glass with his dinner fork. "I'd like to propose a toast," he remarked gallantly. My stomach had been flip-flopping all afternoon, and already, I'd wanted to throw up the shitty appetizers I'd consumed. Hearing his voice certainly didn't help matters any.

"To my parents," he said, raising his glass. "It's so wonderful of them to have us all here together."

There were a few cheers and murmured sentiments. He then clinked his glass with the fork once more and again for good measure. He turned to Amelie. "But the person I especially would like to thank is this woman seated right here next to me." He motioned toward Amelie, and I watched as her face reddened. She smiled nervously as she glanced around the table. All eyes on her.

Are you fucking kidding me? I wanted to kill the bastard. But mostly, I wanted to save her. Only it was too late. Timing never had been our thing.

"This woman... she has brought nothing but immense joy to my life and so..." He trailed off as he pulled a little blue box from his coat pocket. I watched as he bent down and knelt before her. Amelie's hands flew to her mouth. "And so," he raised his voice, "I'd like to ask her to be my wife." What the fuck is this? He's actually proposing with bad poetry? "Amelie," he said opening the box, "will you marry me?" There was dead silence. I'm pretty sure I held my breath. He eyed her expectantly. Until, finally, she answered. And what else could she have said other than... yes.

"No, it's fine, really," I assured her. "I'm taking a cab back." I checked my watch for the fifteenth time in the past five minutes. "It should be here any minute."

By this point, we'd retreated into the garden, away from prying eyes of the crowd. I took her left hand in mine and eyed the ring. "Impressive," I said, letting her hand drop. She stared off into the distance and then up at the sky. It was cold out, the day overcast and grey. She wasn't wearing a jacket, and I wanted to give her mine, but I didn't. Fitting, I thought to myself.

"I'm sorry, Jack," she whispered without looking at me. I followed her gaze and saw that she'd been watching children playing out on the lawn. "I know this has been miserable... and I'm sure there are a thousand other, better ways you could've spent Thanksgiving."

She looked up at me then, and I saw something in her eyes I hadn't seen before. Hesitation.

"Yes, there are. But I wanted to spend it with you."

"And now you have," she choked out.

"And now I have," I said.

"I-I didn't know—"

"It's ok," I murmured, cutting her off.

"Is it?" she asked.

I smiled. "It will be."

I heard someone call out that a cab was waiting out front.

"Are you sure?" she asked again.

I didn't know what she meant. It could have been a lot of

things. Either way, I lied. "Yes, I'm sure," I said, and I pulled her close.

She kissed my cheek and pulled back slowly. "I'll call you."

I nodded, gave her hand one last squeeze, and then I walked away.

This time was easier than the last. For, this time, she'd watched me go.

~

I'D ALREADY BOOKED A RED-EYE FLIGHT FIVE MINUTES INTO the cab ride on the way back to the hotel. I realized instantly that I had to go and that I had to make it quick. Just like ripping off a Band-Aid. So, I went straight back to the hotel room, grabbed my things, and deftly scribbled a note for Amelie.

Sorry but I had to run.

Love,
Jack

P.S. You're an absolute fool if you marry him.

I placed the note on her pillow, and then I hightailed it out of Boston without looking back. If I'd disliked that city before, I surely hated it now.

~

IT WOULD BE SEVEN LONG MONTHS BEFORE I WOULD HEAR Amelie's voice again. Even in my weakest moments, I couldn't force myself to answer her calls—or return them whenever she crossed my mind. Which was a lot. But I was pissed, and I didn't want to hear her shitty excuses. I wanted space. I wanted her to understand that what she did was wrong. That she made the wrong choice by saying yes, by staying—no matter how awkward it might have been if she'd left. Mostly, I wanted her to feel as shitty as I felt.

A few days before Christmas, at the office, I received a card in the mail. I recognized the handwriting immediately, and when I opened it, a small photo fell into my lap. Anxious to read the card, I didn't immediately pick the photo up.

Dear Jack,

I don't know how many other ways I can say it... I'm sorry. And I wish you'd let me explain.

Also, a memento from one of my favorite parts of our trip. I thought you might like to have a copy.

Hope you're well.

Merry Christmas.

Love,
Amelie

I lifted the photo from my lap and studied it. It was a beautiful black and white shot of the old man from the plane and his newborn grandson. She actually did it. I'd thought about that man many times, and I wondered how he was doing. I studied the photo, and while I'm not one for sentimentality, something about the picture got to me. It may have simply been the holidays, or it may have been hearing from her, but

—something about that man's smile reminded me once again of all I didn't have.

Still, I didn't write back and I didn't call. Another email arrived on New Year's Eve.

To: Jack Harrison
From: Amelie Rose
Subject: Running.

Dear Jack,

And here I was thinking that I'd always been the runner—yet look at you showing me up. You know how I hate that.

But I have to say, your skills at both running and ignoring me are rather impressive.

Also, I want you to know that I understand you're angry with me and why. You have every right to be.

But this doesn't mean that I don't miss my best friend. Secondly, last time I checked we were both adults.

Can we start acting like it? Please?

After all, tomorrow marks the start of the New Year.

And I, for one, am hopeful for new beginnings.

Happy New Year, Jack.

Hope you're doing something amazing to celebrate.

Love,

Amelie

This time I couldn't help myself. I wrote back.

To: Amelie Rose

From: Jack Harrison

Subject: RE: Running.

Amelie,

I'm not running... I'm sprinting. ;)

I'm sorry about what happened in Boston. It was a mistake.

As for my unavailability, I apologize. I'm seeing someone and let's just say that she has been keeping me VERY busy. :)

Happy New Year,

Jack

Five minutes after I hit send, she replied. The truth was I was only sort of seeing Jane at the time. But then again, I'd been 'sort of' seeing Jane for a long time. It was all semantics, really.

To: Jack Harrison

From: Amelie Rose

Subject: Sprinting.

Dear Jack,

That is wonderful news.

Tell me about this 'someone'… I'd love to hear about what, or rather, whom is keeping you so busy.

She must be amazing.

I'm so happy for you, Jack.

Talk soon,
Amelie

Dear God. That wasn't the response I'd expected. With Amelie though, it never was. Now that my 'relationships status' had been established, I knew I had to put this thing on pause. Also, I was still angry, angrier than I'd thought, and this whole situation only brought up those feelings. Only I wasn't in the mood to be angry. It was New Year's and I had plans. And Amelie and her shenanigans needed to stay far away from them.

To: Amelie Rose
From: Jack Harrison
Subject: RE: Sprinting.

Amelie,

I will. In time.

For now, we're late for our dinner plans.

Jack

Three weeks later, in one of my weaker moments, I emailed her out of the blue.

To: Amelie Rose

From: Jack Harrison

Subject: What am I doing?

Dear Amelie,

Aside from my dad, I think you're the only one who knows me well enough to answer the questions I'm pondering.

What in the hell am I doing with my life?

You wanted to know about the woman I'm seeing... Well, let me tell you about her...

She's a widow. A widow named Jane. And she has a kid.

A kid, Amelie. A little girl. And you know what? I don't even know if I like kids. That's the shitty part.

I care about Jane. I really do. But I don't know if that's enough. Does that even make sense? I don't know.

I think I could love her. I think maybe I do love her. But I don't know if I'm in love with her. Is there even a difference?

Anyway, I just thought, or maybe I hoped that you'd know the answers. You always did know the right thing to say.

Except when you don't. :)

I miss you,

Jack

Thankfully, she wrote back within a few hours.

To: Jack Harrison

From: Amelie Rose

Subject: RE: What am I doing?

Dear Jack,

Hey stranger.

You're asking me for advice?!? Ha!

Well, it appears you are—so I'll tell you what I think…

Jane sounds nice. I think I remember you liking kids…

But here's the important part: Do not fuck this up.

Either get in or get out.

Easier said than done, I know.

But you have to decide. Because only you can.

Hope this helps,

Amelie

I read her email over and over again. It was exactly what my father had said, only kinder. I could tell she had her guard up —and I knew why. Still, I didn't write back for nearly a week or so, mostly because I didn't know how to respond. Also, I needed to be sure of my position.

To: Amelie Rose

From: Jack Harrison

Subject: I think I know…

Dear Amelie,

What's going on in your life that I shouldn't ask you for advice?

Please tell me that you've slowed down on the drinking. I know you've always been a girl who likes to have fun—but still, I worry.

Also, I need to tell you that you were right about the whole Jane situation. She is nice. And you know what? She's never once asked me for anything, or pressed me for more, and I like that about her.

I still miss you,

Jack

It took Amelie three long weeks to respond, so long that I almost picked up the phone and called. I can't tell you how many times I refreshed my email just to see if her name would suddenly appear. Finally, one day when I'd just about given up hope, it did.

To: Jack Harrison

From: Amelie Rose

Subject: Thinking is not good enough…

Dear Jack,

Sorry for the delay in my response. I've been on location and (quite literally) working my ass off.

No reason to worry, I don't even have time to slow down for a drink these days—although I must remedy that because it does sound nice.

Thinking you know is not good enough. You don't have to have your future all mapped out —but don't play with people's hearts, Jack.

I know I'm not one to speak on the subject of jerking people's hearts around… It's just that if your Jane is a widow, with a kid, then she's already had more than her fair share of that.

Get your shit together, my friend.

Do the kind thing. Love her. Just make sure it's not all for selfish reasons.

Talk soon,
Amelie

I read her email and read it again. I realized how much I hated it when she was right. Especially when it was something that I didn't want to hear. And perhaps I'd been overthinking 'the Jane situation' anyhow. It's not like she was asking for a commitment.

I didn't contact Amelie, and she didn't contact me again for two months following that last email. I'd had enough, and I assumed she had, too. More likely, what else was there to say?

But nine weeks later, I picked up the phone and called her. By then, I'd had enough of playing games. Also, my father died.

10

AMELIE

WHO ENDED UP SAVING WHO?

J flew out of Boston and made it to Austin within fourteen hours of getting Jack's call. I had been shocked to hear about his father. I mean, I knew he'd had heart issues in the past, but I just hadn't expected him to drop dead like that. And quite frankly, I'm sure neither did Jack.

I was as sick as I'd likely ever been on that flight to Texas. My palms were sweaty, I was dizzy, and I'd been unable to keep anything down. I had barely eaten over the previous two days and my whole body ached. It certainly wasn't the best time to be leaving town, but what else could I do? I'd told him when he'd called that I would come. I just hadn't said how soon I'd be arriving.

All I knew was that I had to go. Jack needed me. He wouldn't have called, given everything that had happened, if he didn't. From the airport, I went straight to his apartment, without checking into my hotel to sleep, which is what I'd really wanted to do. What I hadn't accepted was that I was in no shape to help anyone else. At this point, keeping one foot in front of the other seemed to take every bit of energy I had in me. By the time I reached his apartment, I was green, nauseated, and numb. My head was spacey, my timing delayed.

Recently, I'd started a new medication to treat my bipolar disorder. Ian had insisted that it was time I do something to fix 'the problem.' He'd said he knew a doc who would help me, and honestly, I was so desperate to get off the bottle that I probably would have said yes to just about anything. All I knew was that I had sunken to a new, lower, low after last Thanksgiving and the proposal. Ian assured me it was the stress of the wedding—but I knew better. If nothing else, I knew because I hadn't even begun planning the wedding. In fact, one of the reasons that he pressed me to see his doctor friend was so I'd get on the ball and get down the aisle.

By the time I'd arrived at Jack's place, it was after ten p.m. It was warm in Texas, even for June. Much warmer than it had been back in Boston. I remember being covered in sweat as he opened the door. He took one look at me and then threw his arms around me anyway. "Thank you for coming," he said as he pulled back. I gripped his arm to steady myself. "Hey, kid," he said, pulling back just a bit further to take me in. "You look about as shitty as I feel."

"I'm all right." I sighed as I leaned into hug him once more. "Just hot. It's so humid here," I said, wiping the sweat from my forehead.

He took my bag from my less sweaty hand and ushered me inside.

It felt eerie to be there. Ominous almost, even though the apartment was mostly dark save for the light in the kitchen. At first glance, it appeared nothing had really changed. But as I made my way deeper into the living room, so many memories came flooding back, all at once—and it caught me off guard.

Jack watched me stare out the window at the view for a

bit, and then he took my hand and led me down the hall toward his guest room. I recall being too foggy to care to ask why. "Can I get you something to drink?"

My mouth too dry to speak, I shook my head, even though he was in front of me, and I knew he couldn't see. "I got a hotel room." I finally managed to say as he rounded the corner.

He turned. "Don't be silly."

His face looked serious, and my God, I'd missed him, and wow, I was suddenly delirious. "I'm not...I just—"

"I'd like you to stay here."

"Well—" I started to say, but he interrupted with the wave of a hand.

"Well, nothing," he said as he placed my luggage in the spare bedroom. "I need you to stay here."

"Ok," I relented and I eyed his three-day beard. I reached up to touch it. "What's going on here?" I asked in a feeble attempt to lighten the mood.

He pursed his lips. "It's been a rough week."

I took his hand in mine. I wanted to offer him comfort, but also I felt faint. "Tell me all about it," I said, and I led him back to the sofa.

I plopped down and then he sat down beside me. After several moments of silence, he put his feet up and laid his head in my lap. I ran my fingers through his hair and studied his profile as he stared out through the floor to ceiling windows. As we took in the city lights, neither of us spoke. I felt myself beginning to doze off, despite my best intentions. Finally, after several moments, he spoke up, jolting me awake.

"I know we didn't have a conventional relationship—but he was still my father. In large part, he made me the man I am today... and I guess I just...find it hard to believe he's really gone. Without him, you know, there's really no one else." He inhaled, held his breath, and let it out. "I keep sitting here thinking about all of the stuff I'm going to have to change. It's the little things like who's listed as my emergency contact… but it all adds up…you know, and actually—if I'm really honest with myself… it all adds up to nothing. Basically, I have no one."

"That's not true," I tell him. He looked up at me the. His green eyes were piercing and I had trouble breathing.

"Are you ok." He frowned. "You don't look so good."

I squeeze my temples. "I'm fine. I'm just tired."

"Have you been drinking?'

"No!" I say curtly. I shifted and moved away a little, causing him to have to reposition himself. Why do you always assume the worst about me?" I snapped.

He looked taken aback but he left it at that.

"I'm sorry." I finally told him as I placed my hands on each side of his face, forcing him to look at me. When he did, I let out a long, heavy sigh. "I just started new meds, and I'm having a little trouble getting used to them, that's all."

His expression showed surprise and something else, although I wasn't sure what. "What does the doctor say?"

"That I need to give it more time."

"And what do you think… Do *you* think you need to give it more time?"

"I don't know what I think." I exhaled. "If anything—I think I just need to feel better."

"Maybe you should get some sleep. It is late…"

"Yeah. I haven't been sleeping much," I told him without giving it much thought.

"Neither have I."

"I've missed you," I whispered, and I regretted it. I was right on the edge of saying more, of saying something else I'd regret later and I think he knew it.

"I've missed you, too," he says to me with a sigh.

"What do we do about it?" I asked and he squeezed my thigh. Then he turned and buried his head in my stomach, and I could swear he was crying although it was too dark to tell.

"This," he eventually said. "We do this..." he whispered as he wrapped his arms around me.

"And then what?" I asked nonchalantly.

He squeezed tighter. "And then we just hang on..."

"Amelie!" Jack called, trying to shake me awake. "Amelie, wake up." I felt him shake me again. I tried opening my eyes, but all I could see was darkness. "Amelie!" He called once more and I felt his hand on my forehead. "You're covered in sweat."

I felt him touch my arms and then my face but no matter how hard I tried, I couldn't seem to wake up and answer him.

The next thing I remembered was waking up in the hospital.

When I came to, Jack was standing over me, his eyelids red and swollen, dark circles beneath his eyes. I studied his face, or at least tried to as my vision was too blurry to truly focus.

"Hey, kid," he whispered softly smoothing the hair away from my face. My head pounded as I listened to his words roll off his tongue. Jack put his hand on mine, and I could feel the way my teeth chattered and my body shook. After a few minutes, the room came into focus, and I realized how small it was—the gurney taking up at least half of it. "I'm having them bring you another blanket," he said, tucking a blanket beneath my legs. "Snug as a bug in a rug," he whispered and his voice sounded nervous. "I've already had them bring two. Hopefully, we'll get these chills to subside soon."

I watch him while a nurse came in and checked my IV. I winced and he squeezed my hand. "Am I going to die?" I attempted to ask, because that's what I felt like. I tried to get the words out—only my mouth was too dry and my tongue seemed to be stuck to the roof of it, jumbling the words before I could speak them.

"They think you've taken too much medication, Amelie. According to the nurse, the dosage on the bottle of Klonopin you had in your purse was pretty high. Were you taking more than what it said on the bottle?"

I shook my head.

Jack rubbed my hand. "They're running some tests. An EKG... and what not. But you're going to be fine, kid." He scanned the room and watched as the nurse walked out. "Although you sure did give us quite a scare."

"I'm sorry," I tried to say but it came out a mumbled mess.

"I need you to get better..." he told me, his voice abrupt.

I inhaled and it hurt.

"We've got a funeral to plan."

I remembered then about his dad, and I squeezed his hand.

"And you have to promise," he said, his eyes becoming sad. He looked away toward something on the monitor, "to never ever let this happen again."

I swallowed back the tears that were trying to form around the lump in my throat.

"We have too much to do..." he remarked, looking back at me then. "Amelie... I want you to stay with me a while." He swallowed hard. "Until you're better."

I knew he wanted to say that he wanted me to stay until he was better, but he couldn't. That wasn't the kind of man

Jack Harrison could allow himself to be. So, I simply swallowed harder this time, cleared my throat, and wondered how I could possibly say no.

In that moment, I realized, that maybe I needed Jack just as much as he needed me. The only things standing in the way were bad timing, one fiancé, and my soon to be fledging career.

~

11

JACK

IT FELT LIKE LOSING HER ALL OVER AGAIN.

*a*melie and I were cleaning out my dad's house when I found the letters. It happened quite by accident as I hadn't known there'd been more aside from those I had in the book that Amelie had made me way back when. And judging by where they were stashed, I'm not so sure my dad knew about them either. But he's no longer around to ask, so who knows?

I'll never forget what it felt like pulling that first one out of the box and seeing her handwriting. It socked me right in the throat. When I opened it up, it gut-checked me.

Dear Jack,

I write these letters to you while you're napping, or at preschool, or sometimes, you're just sitting on the floor playing, the way you are today. Maybe it's silly, I don't know. Your father seems to think it's a bit overboard, and my friends think I'm crazy, and still, I don't stop. The truth is writing to you makes me feel better—which seems really odd given that you're only three. But the tests show cancer and even though my prognosis is good—well, I just can't help but think, 'what if?' There are all these things I want to tell you about and there's so very much I want to teach you yet. Things other than writing your name and learning using the potty. Bigger things, Jack. And it terrifies me that there's even a possibility that, no matter how small the possibility is right now, I might not be around to teach you these things. I might not get to see you grow up. I don't like to plan for the worst—but then again, death is inevitable, so I figure no matter what anyone else thinks, these letters are impor-tant. They're important to me. And hopefully, they'll be important to you.

Love you always,
Mom

I fold the letter up, return it to its envelope, unfold the next one, and read it, too. All of a sudden, I just couldn't stop reading her words. I felt like for reasons I couldn't—or didn't —yet understand that I really wanted to know her. For the most part, I had always felt such a sense of remorse when it came to my mother. But now, something seemed different— even if I couldn't put my finger on exactly what that thing was.

Dear Jack,

You're sleeping now, your head nestled into my lap. You've come down with chickenpox and you're absolutely miserable. I feel very much the same.
I hate it when you're sick. It's the worst feeling in the world for a mother to watch her child suffer and not be able to fix it. I would do anything to take your misery away and yet I can't. I know

this is just a typical childhood illness and that it'll pass, but it makes me think of all the mother's out there who don't get to be so lucky.

Watching you suffer makes me consider my own illness and how there are some things in life we just can't fix. We can only make the best of them.

Someday, and it isn't a matter of if—but a matter of when you'll come across something you want to fix but can't. Maybe it's a friend or a girlfriend—or maybe it'll be your own babies getting sick. So, I want to give you the same advice I need to hear right now. Just sit with it, Jack. Just be there and make the very best of whatever shitty situation it is you can't fix. Sometimes just holding that person in your arms is the very best answer.

Sometimes, this will fix it—but often it won't. Hold on anyway. Because what else can you do? Having you has taught me this. It has taught me so many things—and the very best of all of them is the power of love.

Love you,
Mom

P.S. Hopefully I don't sound like I'm rambling. This is what tired parents do.

SOMEWHERE AROUND THE FOURTH LETTER OR SO, AMELIE came in and sat down beside me. She handed me a glass of water, and she didn't say anything, which I appreciated.

We just sat there in silence for a long while and stared at the contents of my parent's lives.

Eventually, I drank the water, laid my head in her lap, and cried myself to sleep.

And I'm not a crier.

~

"THERE ARE ALL OF THESE LETTERS MY MOTHER WROTE," I told Amelie the following day, as I flipped through the box I'd just carried from the bedroom to the kitchen. "I found dozens of them I didn't even know we had."

She cocked her head to the side and studied me. She'd been out of the hospital for two days and the color was finally starting to reappear in her cheeks. "That's amazing, Jack," she eventually remarked as she looked through old photos. I've seen them but I'm not ready to really see them.

"I guess," I told her. "But in some ways, it's like losing her all over again."

She nodded, studying a photo. "I can imagine." I watched her face as she moved from photo to photo and I'm worried. I don't tell her this—but I was afraid she was going to leave. I mean, I knew she was going to leave. It's just that I wasn't ready. Not yet.

"You're looking better," I told her in an attempt to fish for the answers to the questions I had, but without having to actually ask them. She looked at me then. "Are you feeling better?" I asked.

She looked away. Maybe she knew me better than I thought she did. "Yeah, I am... Much better..." She sighed, setting the stack of photos on the counter. Then she propped herself up on top of the counter next to the photos.

My dad's kitchen was a wreck by this point. There was food the neighbors had dropped by and neither Amelie nor I seemed to be hungry, so it just sat there. There were half empty boxes and unopened mail. The funeral was to take place the following morning and all I wanted to do was sleep. I didn't want to pack up my dad's things. I didn't want to deal with well-meaning neighbors. I just wanted to be alone with her.

"Hey, Jack," Amelie called and I looked over at her, but she wasn't looking at me. She was focused on something outside the kitchen window. "I know there's a lot going on, and I just want to apologize. I really didn't mean to come here and add to your troubles."

I walked over to the counter where she was perched, and I wedged myself in between her legs. "Are you kidding me?" I asked. "You haven't added to anything." I frowned. "You've actually helped me a great deal…"

She eyed me as she swept her hair up into a bun and wrapped it on top of her head. "It doesn't feel that way," she told me, her eyes sad.

"Well, it is that way," I said taking her chin in my hand, forcing her to look at me.

She bit her lip, paused and then exhaled. "There's something I need to tell you…"

I furrowed my brow, and I waited. "Ok," I urged. Still, she hesitated. "Tell me."

She looked away again and then back at me. As she searched my eyes, she began to smile slightly. "Ah, you know what… never mind."

"You can't do that, Amelie."

She waved her hand and then pushed me backward. Then she hopped off the counter. "No, really, it's nothing," she assured me. "It's just work stuff—and I just decided I don't wanna talk about it."

I watched her as she picked up a plate and wrapped it in newspaper. "When do you have to get back?" I asked.

She shrugged. "How long do you need me to stay?"

Forever, I wanted to tell her. As long as you can, would have been my next best response. Instead, I purse my lips and then relax. "Until you have to go." I compromised.

She looked out the window once more, this time further

off. "I told Ian I'd be a week or so, you know..." she said, chewing on her bottom lip. "He's my boss."

"Your work is important. I get it."

She smiled. "I like to think so. But sometimes I wonder."

I looked away and shuffled through the box of letters. "Well, you shouldn't."

"When has shouldn't ever stopped me before?" she asked, and I heard her laugh, but I still couldn't look at her. For the first time in as long as I could remember, maybe ever, I was scared. Scared of losing the only really good thing I had left. And yet I knew it was just a matter of time before she goes. Worse yet, if she were to stay, it would only be a matter of time before one of us would mess things up, and this time, likely, once and for all.

~

12

AMELIE

WHAT'S IN A GOODBYE?

I was lying there in Jack's apartment in his spare bedroom. I checked the time. It was 2:48 in the morning, and I could hear him in his office down the hall. There was a part of me that wanted to go to him, but there was another part telling me to stay put. His father's funeral was in eight hours, and I highly doubted either one of us would sleep between now and then.

I hadn't really slept in days, not since the hospital. The ER docs told me to discontinue the Klonopin and discuss next steps with my doctor. But I'd been so busy helping Jack and trying to recover from my near death experience, that I'd failed to follow up with my doctor. Also, my doctor so happened to be Ian's good friend, and I really wasn't ready to open that can of worms. Not yet. The only trouble was yesterday. The horrible thoughts I'd had once upon a time, returned unexpectedly. And all I'd been able to think about since was how my life and my career and the only stable relationship—if you could call it that—I'd ever had were all pretty much over. Ian had been fairly understanding—but he also wanted me home. The trouble was I didn't want to go home.

Because the truth was, I wasn't even sure I wanted to live.

I STAYED AT JACK'S SIDE THROUGHOUT THE SHORT SERVICE. HE didn't cry. He just sat there stoically with his hands in his lap. It didn't turn awkward until afterward when everyone assumed we were a couple, although neither of us did much in the way of correcting them.

Following the service, we rode to the cemetery where his father was to be buried next to his mother. I stared out the window at the leaves on the trees, green and lush. As the warm sunlight poured through the tinted window and onto my skin, the only thing I could think of was who might sit at Jack's side at my funeral. I wondered who all would turn out for the occasion. Would it be small and intimate? Or large—teeming with people and their good intentions, glad that if it had to be somebody to die, it wasn't them? Would they be sad for an entire day—or would they pay their respects and get on with it like the rest of the world? Would the day be gray and cloudy, overcast—or gorgeous like today? Almost too gorgeous to hold an occasion with such finality. And how did one really say goodbye anyway? I wondered what I had done in my life—if anything—to deserve the grief of family or friends—or lack thereof, depending on the person, and I couldn't come up with one good thing. Part of me considered what an odd thing this was to think.

While the other part felt nothing.

"Seriously? Why don't you stay for a while?" Jack asked the following morning out of the blue. I was lying on his couch and he was pacing. I hated it when he paced. It wasn't like him. "Take some time off, maybe a sabbatical," he said. I eyed him curiously. The truth was I had already had three, maybe four shots of the vodka I'd picked up the afternoon before. I knew I shouldn't drink, but I also knew I had to make the horrible thoughts go away. "We could go somewhere," he suggested.

I didn't say anything at first. I simply closed my eyes. My heart, I think, if only I could feel any sort of emotion within it, wanted to say yes. So my mind did the speaking. "How did everything get so messed up?" I asked.

I could feel his eyes on me even though I hadn't opened mine. "I don't know. That's life, I guess."

"Then maybe I don't want to live," I said. I didn't mean to say it. Somehow, it just slipped right on out.

In an instant, Jack was at my side. I felt him kneel beside the couch. "WHAT the fuck are you talking about, Amelie?"

"Nothing—" I said as I opened my eyes. I shook my head. "I'm just tired."

"You sound like you've been drinking. You smell—"

"Vodka doesn't have a smell!" I interjected and instantly, I regretted it. But I was drunk, and I wasn't thinking clearly. My defenses were down. I looked over at him. He's got me and we both knew it.

"It's eight o'clock in the morning, Amelie. Why are you drinking?"

"I don't know, "I told him.

"Well, maybe you should give it some thought." I watched as he stood, headed straight for the front door, and let it slam behind him.

I would've left, too. I would have grabbed my things and hightailed it home. If only I hadn't had so much to drink.

I DIDN'T HAVE A DRINKING PROBLEM. REALLY I DIDN'T. WHAT I had was—a not feeling anything, a numbing problem that I would use drinking to fix. And if it wasn't the drinking—then it was the medication– and if it wasn't the medication—then it was my work—and if it wasn't my work—then I hadn't figured out what it was yet. Which scared me. Because I was going to have to. If I stayed in Austin any longer, I was probably going to lose my job. And my fiancé, too. Although that was probably good riddance. But, then again, Ian had his good qualities, too. I drank less when I was with him. Actually, I did all the bad things less. Which really was kind of nice.

I wouldn't want anyone, least of all Jack, to think Ian was all bad. That's why I hadn't told him the whole truth. But does the whole truth always need to me told? In this case, I think not. I mean… sure, Ian was holding something over my head. Sure, I was afraid of that 'very bad thing' I'd done getting out. But as I said, he has his good qualities, too. And anyway, don't we all have something we hold over our lover's head in one way or another? We hold onto it with the very idea that if they screw up we are goners—but first, they're going pay. My mother always said, 'Being in love is like handing your lover a gun and expecting them not to use it.' With Ian, he let me know the gun is loaded. Lots of lovers wouldn't. They'd just shoot. And there is no safety in that.

Ian settled me. He loves me—even though he would show it in his own narcissistic way. I'd begun to consider that maybe there are many types of love. And perhaps these different types show up at different times, depending on what you need and where you're at in your life. I wondered if I was at the point where I needed to settle down with someone who would keep me stable. With someone like Ian. And while I didn't have all the answers… I was getting there.

Speaking of safety and security, Ian sent me an assignment last night. A very special one. He's sending me to Hawaii on assignment. Scheduled to take place three weeks from now, he suggested we just get married while we're there. I didn't tell him yes. About eloping. But I didn't tell him no, either. Because I really want the gig.

"I'm just going to go," I informed Jack when he got back to the apartment. He'd been gone four hours, and by this time, I'd napped and was in the process of sobering up. I told him I was sorry. I apologized for causing him so much added grief when he's already going through so much. He said I hadn't added anything other than help. Then, because I felt so terrible—both about my behavior and about leaving, I leaned in and wrapped my arms around him. And that was when I smelled it. Or rather her. A woman's perfume, and something else, too. Sex. There was no mistaking it once you've gotten wind of it—it is what it is.

I pulled back. "Where were you?" I demanded.

Jack looked at me funny. "I was running errands…"

"You don't smell like fucking errands," I said, and I was angrier than I should have been. This much seems apparent to him.

He backed away and waved his hand in the air. "What are you talking about?' he asked and then he let out a long sigh. "Have you had more to drink?"

And this is when I lost it. "Fuck you, Jack!" I screamed. "Fuck. You." I spat and held up my middle finger for added measure. Maybe I wasn't as sober as I thought. Or maybe I was just enraged. I couldn't quite tell. But the good news was, at least I felt something.

Jack put more distance between the two of us. "I don't understand—"

I crossed my arms over my chest. "Who were you with just now?' I demanded, and I cocked my head to the side. "Where did you go?"

He appeared confused as though I hadn't just asked very precise questions. "I went to Jane's, why?"

"Jane's! Jane's…" I spat. "You went to fucking Jane's?" I crossed the dining room toward him and he looked genuinely afraid

"I don't understand—"

"You don't understand?" I scoffed as I gripped the back of one of his dining chairs and watched the color drain from my knuckles. "Of course, you don't fucking understand!" I yelled.

"Amelie," he said, trying to get a word in. I realized that no, actually, I wasn't drunk at all. I was just pissed.

"So… let me get this straight… you went to Jane's while I'm here, in YOUR apartment putting MY life on hold… and YOU went to Jane's?"

I don't see—"

"Of course, you don't see." I spit out like venom as I unintentionally pulled the chair. It moved. Jack eyed the chair and then me. "Where was JANE when it was time to go through your dad's stuff? Huh? Where was JANE at the funeral?"

"Amelie, I—"

"No! No!" I hissed. "You don't get to give me some sorry excuse this time for why you're just another man who is full of shit."

He scoffed then, and although somewhere deep down I could see he was a little hurt by my words, and I was glad. "Can I speak now?" he eventually said, taking a seat in the chair that put the farthest amount of distance between us. I put all my weight on my hands, leaned forward, and glared at the floor. "Look, I'm sorry," he said quietly. "I just don't like it when you drink."

I didn't look at him. "This isn't about me drinking."

"The truth is—" he exhaled, "is that I don't know what this is about."

"Maybe I'm just crazy. Is that what you want to say? Go ahead, say it. Everyone else does."

He exhaled loudly. "You're not crazy, Amelie."

"Are you sure about that? I take the same medication that crazy people take…"

He deadpanned. "You are not crazy. You're just a little unbalanced."

I threw up my hands. "Well, gee, Jack… when you put it like that, it makes me think that maybe you're right."

"I am right."

"Whatever."

"Speaking of… what's going on with your medication? What are you on and why were you taking so much? You've never really answered my questions…"

"It's complicated," I answered, not wanting to go into it. "But I have to get back to Boston."

I figured he was going to press me further—that he was going to demand answers. I figured that in typical Jack fashion, that he was going to try to fix it.

Only, instead, he said the most unexpected thing. He sighed and then he looked away. "I know," he told me. "That's why I went to Jane's."

~

13

JACK

LOVE IS A GAMBLE.

I retreated to my room, closed the door and shut Amelie out. I showered and wrapped a towel around my waist because actually getting redressed felt like too much work. Then I made my way over to the chair by the window, which overlooked downtown, facing west. I sat back in it, and I ran my fingers through my still damp hair and then over my face. It was dusk on a beautiful summer day and as I looked out over the city, I considered how many times I'd sat in this very position and thought about the very woman who is now sitting in my living room.

Suddenly, everything seemed so close and yet so very far away. I stayed that way for a long while, and I thought about Jane and what going to her house meant. I wished that I could take it back although I knew I couldn't. Jane is kind. She is a good woman and a decent lover—but she isn't and never would be enough. Half of me wanted to be ok with this, always. To bide my time, to not want anything more, to be glad that she didn't ask for it—but there was the other half who wanted to settle for nothing less than exceptional. There was the part of me that understood what my father would have said had he still been here and that was you can't live an exceptional life by settling for anything less. As I watched the daylight fade, I suddenly began to wonder what my mother would've said. And then I remembered the letters.

I went to the closet where I'd stashed the box I had brought over from my father's house. I opened it carefully and pulled an envelope out. I ran it through my fingers, but something told me it wasn't the right one so I placed it back. I did the same with another, and then another. The fourth letter I flipped over and realized that it was numbered on the back in small print. I found it odd that I hadn't noticed this before, but this particular number was smudged, and the blotted ink caught my eye. Also, looking back, I realized the letters at least up until that point, and maybe even after, felt foreign to me. They felt like touching the ghost of a person that I wasn't sure I was ready to remember. I never looked at them eagerly. Instead, I considered them like one might consider a scab. Picking it is never a good idea. Picking at it only leads to scars. It would be a long time before I realized that scars are also a part of the healing process and that they are ok. Necessary, even. It would take seeing someone else's to finally hammer that home. I swallowed, returned to my chair, and opened up the letter numbered eighty-nine.

Dear Jack,

Today is your first day of kindergarten. I am up early to make your lunch and to make all of the other necessary preparations—but I thought I'd take a quick moment to write to you.
When your first and only child starts school—it is a big deal. I don't know how other mothers feel, but for me, this will be a diffi-cult day. Maybe other mothers have other children at home—other children yet to have their first days of kindergarten. But I never

will. The moment they found the cancer when you were just eight months old, I knew that you would be my one and only. I felt it in my bones even if I hadn't yet learned to believe it. That's the thing about the big truths in life, Jack. If you're paying attention, you'll almost always feel them before you're ready to see them.

It is hard to imagine that five years have passed since you came into our lives. In some ways, it's hard to imagine ever having lived this life without you. Yet, in others, it seems your father and I were just exiting that hospital parking lot, looking at each other and asking 'what now?'

Well, our 'what now' is that you will walk into that school and take your seat at the desk labeled with your name, and you will act as though you were never supposed to do anything else. You are ready while I am not. But this is your nature. You were born ready. No matter what challenge has ever come your way I have watched you excel at feeling out the next right thing to do. You don't ask 'what now.' You're a doer. A feeler. You always have been. And I hope you always will be.

So, with that I will let you go this morning with greater ease than I'd like. I will watch as your little hand slips out of mine, long before I am ready, and long before we get to the place where it's time to say goodbye. You know what you are supposed to do. And if ever in life you find yourself questioning 'what now' or, more importantly, what the right thing is—well, that's how you know it's time to let go and feel your way through.

Love you always,
Mom

~

SEVERAL LETTERS LATER, I CLIMBED INTO BED. I'D WANTED TO go and speak to Amelie and make things right again—but I didn't have the energy to actually force myself to do it. More importantly, I wasn't sure what to say—or if anything good would come from a conversation between us at this point. In part, it killed me that I was being such a coward. It wasn't my style, and yet here I was. Now, I just wanted sleep. It would take me a long time to understand that sometimes the best way to win a fight is not to fight at all. This was just the first time of many that I'd try this theory on for size.

Sometime between falling asleep and dawn, I heard the creak of my bedroom door, the sound it made only when it was being opened slowly and cautiously. I listened as the familiar footsteps made their way to my bed. A part of me expected that she'd come, which was in large part what made me ok with not going to her. She pulled back the covers and climbed into bed. I felt the coolness of her body as she scooted closer to mine, all but forcing me to spoon her.

"What time is it?" I asked. She tensed and I realized she hadn't known I was awake.

"After three," she whispered into the dark.

She reached for my hand and pulled it over her body. Then, as she attempted to scoot backward into my chest as though there'd been any room left between us, she said softly, "Jack? There's something I need to ask you...."

Amelie hadn't given me time to brace for impact. In fact, she'd hardly paused at all. The words spilled out as though she'd been holding them in and just couldn't contain the question any longer.

"Do you think I should marry him?" she asked. The question hung between us, in the darkness, quickly filling the room, and breaking my heart.

"I don't know," I eventually told her. It was the best I could do.

""No," she said quietly, "I hadn't figured you would."

"Then why did you ask?"

"I'd hoped you might."

I squeezed her just a little and sighed. "Can we talk about it the morning? I'm really tired."

She squeezed back. "My flight leaves at ten."

I wrapped my arms around her tighter. And I left it at that. There would be plenty of time for letting go later.

THE MORNING LIGHT POURED IN ALTHOUGH I HAD ALREADY been awake for hours. My arm had fallen asleep underneath the weight of Amelie, but she looked so peaceful, I hadn't wanted to wake her by moving it. I laid that way for a while watching her expression as she slept. At some point, she stirred awake. I bit her earlobe. "What time is it?" she asked, breathing heavily.

"Early."

"Did I miss my flight?"

"No," I assured her.

"That's too bad," she said and she flipped over, buried her head in my chest, and fell back asleep.

"IF YOU DON'T WANT TO GO, THEN WHY ARE YOU GOING?" I asked as we pulled into the airport parking lot. I'd purposely waited as long as possible to ask in order to see if she might bring it up. I wasn't going to push her to stay. It took forever for me to find an open spot and about as long for her to answer. As I turned off the ignition, she finally did. She looked at me incredulously. "I have a job."

"I have one, too," I assured her.

"You don't have a boss, Jack."

"Sure I do. They're called investors."

She shot me a look that conveyed annoyance and then she shook her head. "It's not the same."

"You can take pictures from anywhere. Why not here?"

"Well, for starters, the magazine I'm employed by is based out of Boston. I have a home there—and a life—"

"I'm not asking for forever. Just a little longer..." And there it was. Even though I'd promised myself I wouldn't do it. She'd forced my hand. I asked her to stay.

Amelie exhaled and focused her attention out the passenger window. "I'm just not in a place where I can walk away from it all."

"I'm not asking for you to walk away."

She turned then. "What are you asking for?"

I swallowed. "I don't know. Just a little more time."

"I do love him, Jack."

"I'm sure you do."

Her face fell. "Then why are you asking me to stay? Especially, when I'm the one who stands to lose the most?"

"If you want to get on that plane, then by all means go. But—if you're doing it because you think you have to—then I think you're making a mistake."

She sighed then, and I knew the sound. It was a sigh of defeat, mixed with annoyance at my being right.

Amelie stared out the window and neither of us spoke for several minutes until suddenly, I had a brilliant idea.

"What if I drove you back?"

She glared at me, her mouth hanging open, and I recognized it instantly. She liked my idea. Although she wasn't ready to admit it.

"We can take the long route—a detour."

"I have to be in Hawaii in fifteen days," she exclaimed as she pursed her lips.

"So we'll take fourteen. Or thirteen. Whatever you need."

"But—"

"Ah, come on. A road trip… Think about it. It'll be like old times…"

She cocked her head. "Where will we go?"

"Anywhere. Who cares?"

"Well, for one, my boss will."

"Make it about work." I could see her thinking, her mind working hard at fitting the pieces together. But Amelie was too pure to ever be as good a liar as I was. So I decided to just hand it to her. "Tell him we're going to spread my dad's ashes and that you're going to do a piece on the best places across the US to do that sort of thing."

She frowned. "Your dad was buried. In the ground."

"Yeah," I agreed. "But what's-his-name doesn't know that."

She slapped my arm. "You're crazy, Jack Harrison."

"There are conditions, though…" I told her as I raised a brow. I said this only after I knew she was in.

She ran her fingers through her long blonde hair, sweeping it away from her face. "Oh?"

"We are going to make a bet."

I eyed her as she wrapped a strand of hair around her finger nervously. Then she grinned and eyed me expectantly.

I delivered my answer without skipping a beat. "On this trip, we're together."

Her face twisted and she released her hair. "What else would we be?"

"No, I mean we're a couple. Full out. No bullshit."

"I'm engaged, Jack," she scoffed.

"Maybe so." I shrugged. "But for the next fourteen or thirteen or however many days, we're going to pretend that you're not."

She crossed her arms. "What does that even mean?"

"It means that we're just together. Whatever happens, happens. We don't fight it. And we don't ask questions."

Amelie threw her head back and laughed. "You're funny,"

she said and then she sat straight up and glared at me. "And then what?"

"And then, at the end of it—if you're happy, well, then you'll have the answer to the question you asked about marrying what's-his-name."

She watched my face for a moment and then bit her lip. "Do I have another option?"

"Yes," I told her with conviction. "To get on that plane and spend the rest of your life wondering what might have happened if you hadn't.

~

14

AMELIE

DID HE KNOW I WAS GOING DOWN?

*I*t had been eighteen minutes since I'd agreed to Jack's bet, and we'd shaken on it. Our first stop so he could throw some clothes in a bag was back to Jack's place. Also, he insisted that we take his Jeep so we ended up swapping vehicles. As we were about to leave, as he was checking to ensure for the third time that he'd packed everything, I watched as he shook his head, and then he casually mentioned he needed to grab the box of his mother's letters. I didn't ask questions, but I also didn't tell him that I'd been studying my dead father's poetry and had been considering trying my hand at some of my own.

I wanted to tell him then, but I didn't, not only because I wasn't ready, but mostly because I'm not very good. And if I were any good, he'd be the first person I'd want to share it with, but I'm not. I'd only written a few things here and there, but my life was such a jumbled mess right then, especially where my thoughts and feelings were concerned, so I figured it couldn't hurt to try and put a few of them on paper.

I texted Ian to tell him that he won't need to pick me up

from the airport, as I'd be driving back. When he immediately called and demanded to know what was going on, I sent the call to voicemail and then texted back that if he wanted me to meet him in Hawaii, then he'd just have to understand that this was something I had to do. Then I pitched Jack's idea about scattering ashes—without telling him that it was Jack's idea, of course—or that the pitch was optional—I reiterated that it was something that I had just decided I needed to do. In the end, he didn't respond back, and I wasn't sure whether or not that was a good or a bad thing.

Our second stop was to the Quick-E Mart to fuel up where Jack pumped the gas while I went in to purchase enough snacks to feed the both of us six times over. I pretty much grabbed two of everything, plus a map. As I was waiting in line to pay, I glanced outside and noticed Jack leaning against his Jeep, his hands stuffed in his pockets. He was staring at something off in the distance, his expression contemplative. Although his gaze gave nothing away, one way or the other, I wondered if he felt as mixed up as I did. As I was ushered up to the counter, I pushed the thoughts aside and reminded myself that I should be excited. I reminded myself to let the anxiety go. Then I exhaled and considered what a perfect day it was for a fresh start. The sky was cloudless, the sun bright—it wasn't yet too hot, and the day was ours for the taking.

~

AS WE PULLED OUT OF THE GAS STATION, JACK LOOKED OVER AT me casually and grabbed the bag of Sour Patch Kids from my lap. "I need to stop at a sporting goods store on our way out of town."

I asked him what for.

"We're going to camp out," he informed me, popping a

green Sour Patch Kid, his favorite flavor, into his mouth. I knew this because he'd mentioned as much each and every single time he had picked a green one out of the bag. I glanced at him sideways and then clapped in excitement. "I love camping!"

Only at this point, it hadn't yet occurred to me that Jack and I might possibly have completely different ideas of what camping actually was.

INSIDE THE MASSIVE TWO-STORY SPORTING GOODS STORE, JACK gripped the basket as though his life depended on it. He was in his element, refusing to give even the slightest bit of control. Although I didn't yet know the half of it. I remarked that I'd never seen so much stuff—all dedicated to sleeping outside. Jack ignored me and before long, he was throwing handfuls of stuff into the cart, just the way I had back at the convenience store.

We hadn't even made it through the halfway point in the store when I stopped mid-aisle and surveyed the contents of our cart, which by then was filled a little more than halfway. "This seems like a lot of stuff," I commented, picking up a flare. Jack stopped, shrugged, and continued up the aisle.

"Why do we need flares?" I inquired refusing to follow.

He stopped, searched my eyes, and walked backward to where I was standing. He gently took the flares from my hand and tossed them back into the basket. Then he leaned in and kissed my cheek. He pulled away and his eyes met mine. "Because I say we do."

I sighed and he took me by the hand, grabbed the tail end of the cart, and continued to move along.

He did not, however, refrain or slow down his process of stuffing items in the cart.

"I'm no expert—" I said, "but I really don't think camping requires all of this—"

"Well, I am an expert," he replied, studying the nine thousand varieties of sleeping bags the store stocked on their shelves. There are seriously rows and rows of sleeping bags. I glanced at the price tag on the one he was eyeing, as the thought crossed my mind that I might not have a job to go back to when this is all said and done.

"Why don't we share a sleeping bag?" I suggested.

Jack looked over at me and smiled. "That could work," he smirked taking two off of the shelf, "but it's always best to be prepared."

I placed my hands on my hips and decided, at that point, I'd had enough. "Obviously, you've never been poor!"

Jack looked over at me slowly, furrowed his brow, and then quickly turned his attention back to one more thing we didn't need sitting on the shelf.

"I hate to tell you this," I said removing several items from the cart, "you know, sadly a large portion of the world's population lives in tents… or less, even."

I watched as he fished something out of his pocket, which turned out to be the keys to the Jeep. He didn't take his eyes off mine as he walked over to where I was standing, took the items from my hand, and placed them back in the cart. Then he turned my hand over, placed the keys inside my palm, and closed my fingers around them without ever taking his eyes from mine. "I think you should wait in the car."

I rolled my eyes.

Jack smiled curtly. "We'll be on our way sooner that way, I assure you."

"Fine," I said attempting to hand over my credit card.

He laughed, shook his head, and walked back toward the shelf. "I don't want your money, Amelie.

I felt my face grow hot. "Jack… just one question…"

He looked over his shoulder briefly.

"Just what in the hell are we going to do with all of this stuff—after the trip?"

He'd turned so I could only make out his profile, but I swore I saw a slight grin play across his face. "We'll use it for next time."

And there it was—I'd used the word 'we' and now, so had he. Not only that—but he'd insinuated a future between the two of us. I turned and stormed out of the store. Once outside, I perched myself on the curb and rested my chin on my knees. I hugged them in tight. My heart pounded, and I realized all along, my unease had little to do with the number of items Jack was putting in the shopping cart—or even our different ideals of what camping entailed—and everything to do with the fact that he saw a future between us that I wasn't sure existed.

Eventually, I made my way back to the Jeep where I waited for Jack to finish purchasing nearly every item in the entire store. After twenty minutes, and he still hadn't emerged, I was even more restless than I'd been sitting on the curb. I considered taking a nap—only the thoughts in my head wouldn't stop coming. My mind raced, I was bored, and the walls of that tiny Jeep started to feel like they were closing in on me.

If my current situation was any indication of how things would play out, I realized that this was going to be one hell of a trip. It was with that thought that I reached into the backseat to grab a bottle of water and noticed the box of letters sitting there. My curiosity piqued. The next thing I knew, I was carefully opening the box, and pulling out one of his mother's letters. As I held it in my hands, I considered whether or not I should open it. But, eventually, boredom and curiosity won out over any good conscience I might have had. I removed the note from its envelope, looked out the window toward the store, and without seeing Jack, I began to read.

Dear Jack,

I'm sick today, but I wanted to make sure I got a letter in while you're at school—and I still mostly have a few shreds of energy left to put pen to paper. They're playing with my medication, and it's making me feel very off. This is why I feel so terrible. That's perhaps the saddest thing of all. It's not even the cancer doing it. I decided yesterday that I no longer want to take this particular medication anymore. It's a trial drug anyhow, and your father is furious at me. He says I'm not trying hard enough. In moments such as these, I hate him, Jack. I really do. How can he possibly not see how hard I'm trying? I'm trying so hard, son. But I just can't stand to feel like this every waking second of the day. The cancer may beat me, at some point—but I can assure you, the medication never will. I refuse to trade being dealt one shitty hand for another. So, while I'm angry with your father for insisting that I continue the meds, I understand that he loves me and just wants me to get better. It would be easy for me to take my anger about having cancer on him just as he's taking the fact that he's afraid out on me. Fear is a very powerful thing, Jack. But only if you allow it to be. It is with this sentiment that I want to tell you about handling disagreements. Not just any disagreement either—I'm particularly talking about the big ones. Because the more something matters— the bigger the fight. And the bigger the fight, the bigger the hurt— and the more each of you stand to lose. You have to really understand your opponent and whether or not they're really your opponent at all. You have to understand what they have to lose. And if you can do that—if you can see their fear and their hurt for what it is—then you can come out on top.

However, coming out on top doesn't necessarily equate to winning. Often, it simply means minimizing the damage. And while winning is fun... in love, the stakes are typically too high to declare a clear-cut champion. More on this later, my hand hurts, and my heart is heavy.

I love you, Jack. And I continue to fight, for you—and for your father.

Love,
Mom

I TUCKED THE LETTER BACK IN THE ENVELOPE AND CAREFULLY placed it back in its rightful spot in the box, making sure not to disturb others in the process. When I looked up again, I could see Jack pushing an overly filled cart my direction. But my mind wasn't on him, or the goods he'd purchased.

It had been well over a week since I'd taken any medication to treat my bipolar disorder, and I was beginning to feel the effects of my own illness more deeply. After reading Jack's mother's words, I suddenly felt as though there might be no end in sight. This wasn't the first time I'd found myself in this predicament. Most of my life I'd felt like I was walking a tightrope of being ok, and then instantly not. In the past, I had gone long periods without taking medication at all, but each and every time I quit, I ended up in really bad shape. This time, I was terrified. I could suddenly see that the deck was stacked against me—as though my future was a house built of cards, ready to crumble at any time—it only took a storm, with its wind blowing hard enough to knock me down. Which it inevitably would. I looked up to see Jack standing there waiting for me to unlock the door. Looking at him then, I began to think the storm that would take me out had a name—and it was Jack Harrison.

By the time we pulled out of parking lot of the sporting goods store, it was well after one p.m. Jack didn't mention the fact that I was crying. He didn't ask what was wrong, and I didn't volunteer to tell him. He'd simply loaded the contents into the rear of the Jeep, got in, and suggested that we head to New Mexico to see Carlsbad National Caverns. He spoke of the time that his parents had taken him there when he was about five years old and how he'd always wanted to go back. He asked me if I'd ever been, and he smiled when I told him I hadn't. When he asked if I opposed the idea, I simply shook my head. Because, the truth was, I couldn't think of a better first stop than a giant hole in the ground in which I could descend into.

15

JACK

THE DEEP END.

"*A*re you sure you don't want to go for a swim?" I asked once more. We'd decided against camping as it was well after dusk by the time we arrived. We checked into the hotel late, after nine p.m. And I'd been trying to get Amelie out of bed and down to the pool since we'd checked in an hour ago. The moment we arrived to the room, she'd plopped herself down on the bed and stared up at the ceiling. In fact, she had hardly spoken at all the entire way from Texas to New Mexico.

"Amelie," I called again. She looked over at me. "Put on your swimsuit and let's go."

She stood abruptly and threw her hands up. "Fine," she said eyeing me sideways. "But first there's something I have to tell you."

I sat back on the bed and mentally prepared myself. I knew that tone well. I crossed my arms and waited.

She swept her hair back and pulled it into a ponytail. "I'm not taking any medication," she said grabbing the hair tie from her wrist with her teeth.

"Ok," I told her, I didn't know what else to say. If I were to be honest, I would have told her she didn't need the medication anyway. At the same time, I wasn't an expert—and I didn't know the extent of her feelings or her situation.

"The medication I had been taking...that made me so sick..." she said before trailing off.

I nodded and prodded her to go on, but it took several moments as though she were trying to work out the right words to say.

Amelie waved her hand in the air. "Well, it's just that I'm not sure that I like the doctor, and I know I didn't like that medication..."

"So find another, if you think you need it."

"It's not that simple, unfortunately. Finding a doctor and having that doctor prescribe medication that alters the chemicals in your brain takes a bit of time and effort, Jack."

"I get that. But I'm not sure I'm following you..."

"You know what? Never mind. I'm not even sure I'm following myself."

"Maybe you're just overthinking it," I said, slipping on my swim trunks.

I paused and watched her dig through her suitcase, which in typical Amelie fashion was a horrible mess. "You're probably right," she eventually answered. She'd found her suit in the heap of other clothing she had, and by this point, I was hoping she'd change right where she was standing. Instead, she walked to the bathroom, only partially closing the door. "Oh, and Jack," she called out. "There's something else—" She peered around the bathroom door smashing her unfastened bikini top against her chest.

I didn't answer, but I didn't take my eyes off of hers. I assumed she was going to ask for help with her suit.

"I read one of your mother's letters. I'm sorry—" she said.

I swallowed, realizing that I'd assumed wrong.

IN THE POOL, I SWAM A COUPLE OF LAPS TO BLOW OFF STEAM while Amelie remained on the edge with her feet in the water, watching me. We were the only ones in the pool area as technically, it was closed at this hour. But when I'd slipped the hotel staff member a twenty, he promised to pretend we weren't there. It was with this thought that I slipped back underneath the water. I thought back over one of my mother's letters in particular. As I recalled her words, I swam lap after lap until I had almost nothing left.

Dear Jack,

I thought it was time I wrote to you about ethics. Yesterday, you stole a pack of gum from the grocery store, and as I drove you back to that store to return your stolen goods and apologize, I had the talk with the four-year-old version of you about right and wrong. When your father got home, and I explained the day's events to him, he was appalled at the both of us. It hadn't been enough, in his opinion, to merely offer an apology and return the gum. He wanted you to understand what it took to earn it—so that you'd never need to take anything that wasn't yours again. In turn, he loaded the three of us back in the car, and on the drive back, I considered his position, and I thought about how that same lesson might manifest when you're older. This both amused and terrified me.
Your father had old Mr. Owen, our local grocer, to teach you about mopping floors and bagging groceries and wiping down shelves. Basically, he volunteered your services for a good two hours. But as further punishment, you still didn't get the gum. Your father's tough like that.
I hope that his toughness combined with my not so toughness will have taught you something to save for the future. People will often

let you get away with more than you should. But it takes a bigger man to stand up and teach you the most valuable lessons in life. I hope you're tough like your father, in the sense that you always go the extra mile. Also, never take what isn't yours to take. Work for it. Earn it. It may not be the easiest route, but it's certainly the most satisfying one. The things in life one has to work hardest for are the things that are most worth having.

Love,
Mom

∾

"I KNOW YOU'RE ANGRY WITH ME, AND I'M SORRY," AMELIE whispered, wrapping her legs around my waist. I ran my hands along them and then down her sides and then stopped myself. She'd finally decided to join me in the water, of course, now that I was spent. "Take me to the deep end," she begged as she buried her face against my neck. I pulled back and then quickly took her by the wrists and unwrapped her from around me until she stood there, her expression full of surprise at my separating the two of us. "I'm not angry..." I told her.

"Well, obviously you are…"

I slowly shook my head and glanced toward the other end of the pool. "If you want to go to the deep end, then you're going to have to swim there yourself."

Her cheeks grew red. If there was anything Amelie hated most—it was being told no. "You know what… just forget it," she called over her shoulder as she high-stepped her way back to the edge of the pool.

"I knew you wouldn't do it," I offered, backstroking my way to the deep end. I don't know exactly what it was I was suddenly so irritated about—other than the fact that the writing was on the wall. I was over her and her expectation that she could have whatever she wanted—how she wanted it. Perhaps being confined with someone in a vehicle for nine hours will do that to a person. Make them see the light, that is.

Amelie heaved herself back up onto the side of the pool. "What's your point anyway? If you're not mad then why are you acting like such as ass?" she called out.

"You can't just expect that everyone is going to do what you want whenever you want it, Amelie. Some things you actually have to work for, you know."

"I still don't get your point."

"Forget it—I guess I just wanted to see whether you wanted to go to the deep end badly enough."

"If I did—don't you think I'd already be there by now?"

I smirked. "You nailed it—that's my point, exactly. You want to swim—yet you don't want to put the effort in. You know what happens when you do that in a pool, Amelie? You drown."

She looked away, dismay clearly written across her face.

Eventually, she got over herself and got back in the water. Although simply to prove a point, she never did make it to the deep end.

LATER, AFTER WE'D GOTTEN BACK TO THE ROOM, AND I HAD showered and changed, I pulled out the box of my mother's letters. Then I sat, reading a few, as I waited for Amelie to get showered and dressed. Suddenly, I was desperate not to fight anymore. After reading my mother's words, I realized the last thing I wanted to do was ruin the trip. It's interesting how reading a dead woman's words can teach you about how fleeting life is. So, when Amelie emerged from the bathroom,

I was determined to make things right. So I called her over to my double bed.

"I'm not angry at you," I said, motioning for her to sit down. "You're welcome to read these anytime." She sat down and eyed me hesitantly.

"I know I should have asked first…"

"It's not a big deal," I assured her as I opened the letter and handed it to her. "I really like this one."

She eyed me cautiously and then turned her attention to the letter. I couldn't take my eyes off of her as she read.

Dear Jack,

There are lots of ways to get what you want in this world. Some ways are apparent and some are only apparent to a few. Your father has taught me to be one of those few. You probably won't be at an age for a very long time before you understand there's a method to his madness—so allow me to explain.

There was a cancer specialist/surgeon I wanted to see early on in my treatment. I was informed I needed to get on his waiting list because, due to the fact that he is so good, the wait time to see him is upwards of six months. I did as I was told by my doctor and scheduled an appointment.

Only, when I told your father about the appointment, he was livid. I don't know that I'd ever seen him so angry with me. As he paced across our kitchen floor, back and forth, back and forth, as he was tethered to the wall by the phone cord, he scolded me. This is life and death, he chided—smoke practically blowing out of his ears. I tried to tell him about the waitlist and how it wasn't my fault that the appointment was six months away—but he wouldn't hear any of it. Rules, and waitlists, and stupid excuses, do not apply, he said into the phone, when his wife's life was at stake. And after a while, when it seemed he was getting nowhere with the nurse—he pulled out a trick I hadn't even considered.

"Ask Dr. Clark if he'd be willing to see my wife after hours for an additional stipend," he said. "I'm willing to pay off hour's fees, whatever those may be. Find out and call me back ASAP," he ordered. I sat there my mouth agape. "You can't just pay off the doctor," I told him. "We don't have that kind of money."

"I'm not paying him off," he remarked. "I'm getting your foot in the door. And we're bloody hell not going to wait six months to go by for it to happen either. Some things you wait for. And some you make happen."

To my surprise, Dr. Clark's nurse called back fifteen minutes later offering me an appointment the following week. I couldn't have known it then, but your father's persistence, his unwillingness to give up, added at least three years to my life. The one hundred and fifty dollars extra we paid to see the surgeon sooner rather than later paid for itself a thousand times over. It bought me time.

That day, I learned to act quickly. Especially where it matters. Do not take no for an answer just because someone tells you it once, or twice, or three times. Find another way. You'll be surprised at how often it's worth it.

Love you,
Mom

~

AMELIE STARED AT THE LETTER. I STARED AT HER. EVENTUALLY, she placed it on the nightstand with a sigh. Then she did something I hadn't expected. She turned, crawled toward me, and leaned in and kissed me full on. And I swear it was the most erotic kiss I think I'd ever had. I wanted more, and I tried to get it—but instead, she pushed me backward onto the bed and moved over me, inch by inch. With each kiss, my breath grew more and more rapid until all I could hear was the drum of my heartbeat reverberating between my ears.

When she got to my collarbone, I noticed she was smiling. Not to be one-upped, I sat up and flipped her over onto her back. She eyed me cautiously, but there was also something in her expression that said please don't stop. So I didn't. I returned the favor and then some.

Afterward, when I could breathe normally once again, I looked over at her. She was still smiling. "What in the hell was that?" I asked.

She met my gaze. "I took your mother's advice and learned to act quickly. She was a smart woman..."

"Yeah..." I swallowed, and then I turned my attention to the ceiling.

Amelie rolled over onto her side, took my face in her hands, and kissed me the way she had before. Then she pulled back and said, "And she was right, too. It was totally worth it."

I smiled then. I couldn't help myself.

16

AMELIE

NO ONE EVER TAUGHT ME TO STAY.

*T*he following morning, we packed up and headed to Carlsbad Caverns, which turned out to be way more interesting than I figured it would be. Once we'd made our way through the cave, we decided to make the 750 foot ascent back up to the light of day by elevator instead of making the trek back up the same way we'd come down. As we stepped into the elevator, Jack took my hand and squeezed tight. I looked around at the other cave-goers and then I looked up at Jack. I don't know quite what made me say it other than perhaps I just figured it was time. "Why did you leave South America?"

Jack cocked his head, clearly caught off guard by the question. He glanced around the elevator and then back at me. "You want to discuss this now?

My bottom lip jutted out and I shrugged. "The guide said it would take a full minute to reach the top…"

"This conversation will take longer than a minute," he remarked, his smile small and fixed.

"Have you got anywhere else to be?"

He shook his head and exhaled. "No."

"Well…"

Jack shifted his weight from one foot to the other and looked down at me. Eventually, he sighed quietly. "No one ever taught me to stay."

I sucked in as much air as I could possibly muster in such a tiny space. And I realized that Jack and I suffered the same affliction.

No one had ever taught us to stay.

FROM NEW MEXICO, WE HEADED STRAIGHT UP INTO Colorado. Neither of us had traveled that particular route before, and it took us nearly double the time it should have, as not only was I in charge of the map, but I insisted on taking the scenic route and stopping every time something piqued my interest in order to take photos. Jack never complained although I could tell he hadn't particularly enjoyed giving up control. It's one reason he insisted on doing the driving. Which was fine by me. Mostly, though, neither of us really spoke a whole lot save for a little small talk here and there. It was a comfortable silence.

At one of our stops, Jack took my hand and asked me to follow him to a bench. He pointed and I sat. I knew what was coming. And it wasn't small talk. "What's going on with you and what's-his-name?"

I furrowed my brow. "I thought we were keeping this light and fun?"

"I want to know what I'm getting myself into."

"That's not fair, Jack."

"Why not?"

"I'm not asking you about Jane."

"You can if you want. In fact, I'll just tell you straight up. Jane is great—but there's no future there."

I sighed and looked away. "Tell me something I don't know…"

"Like what?"

My mouth twisted. "I don't know. I just don't want to have this conversation."

"I saw your phone, Amelie. I saw the twenty-five missed calls."

"And?"

"Why are you avoiding it all?"

"I'm not. I'm keeping it light and fun."

"No, you're running."

"You asked me to take this trip with you. So here I am. I don't see it as running."

"Are you going to marry him?"

"I don't know."

"What the fuck is there not to know? It's a lifelong commitment we're talking about here, Amelie. It shouldn't be that hard to say—"

"There's a lot you don't understand," I said, cutting him off.

"Then help me understand. Make me understand. Because I care about you. I've always cared about you…"

"I know."

He waited.

"Look—it's complicated. And I'd rather not complicate our time together by rehashing all of the complication. You said this was supposed to be fun, Jack."

"Who's not having fun?"

I laughed and looked in the direction of the Jeep, then back at him. I raised my brow. "What do you say we climb into the backseat and keep it simple?"

He grinned. "I can do simple. Just not forever…"

I looked in the direction of the Jeep. "Nothing lasts forever, Jack."

JACK AND I WERE IN THE MIDDLE OF THE QUICK LITTLE backseat rendezvous I'd suggested when I just happened to catch something flicker out of the corner of my eye. "Oh, my God."

He didn't stop thrusting, so I sunk my teeth into his shoulder. Hard.

"Ow. What the fuck?" He hissed as he moved into me once more.

"Stop!" I shrieked.

Later, he would ask since when had 'oh my God' meant stop—but in that moment, he simply asked why.

"Look," I demanded, pointing my finger. "There's an entire Asian tour group watching us."

It took a second for him to spot them. "I think they're taking pictures," I said, my voice low.

Jack thrust into me.

"What are you doing?" I squealed trying to climb off. He held me in place. "The windows are tinted. They can't see us," he whispered, adjusting my hips.

"They're taking pictures. I don't think your Jeep is that cool."

He grinned as he took my breast into his mouth and pushed into me softly. "Then we better give them a show."

"Jack, this illegal."

"Don't worry, I'll be quick," he promised.

And he was.

FOLLOWING OUR QUICK LITTLE BACKSEAT SIDESHOW, WE headed into Colorado. One thing that always amazed me about road trips was how quickly the landscape changes. It could go from dry and barren to lush and green seemingly instantly. This is how it was for Jack and I, too. Somewhere just over the state line, I decided to prove my point.

"You do realize that what's-his-name is my boss, right?"

Jack didn't answer. He didn't have to. I watched his jaw set and harden.

"If I fuck this up, I lose my job."

"There are other jobs out there…"

I turned in my seat and did a double take. "I love my job!"

"Yeah, but do you love him?"

I stared at him for a moment, my mouth no doubt hanging open. When he turned and raised an eyebrow at me as though to signal that I'd forgotten that he was awaiting a response, I shifted my entire body to face the passenger side window. "You're quite audacious today," I eventually said crossing my arms.

He looked over at me, one brow raised. "I was hoping it'd rub off on you."

"Fuck you, Jack."

A smile played across his face and then I watched it fade. "You just did."

ACCORDING TO THE MAP ON MY PHONE, WE WERE A LITTLE LESS than two hours out from the hotel I'd booked in a small mountain town. Jack had still refused to camp although he wouldn't give reasons as to why. As for me, I alternated between staring out the window and staring at my phone. Anything to avoid talking to him. Ian and I had been texting back and forth. I'd sent him a few shots I'd taken, and it seemed he'd warmed up to the idea of the road trip by this point. Oddly enough, the angrier I got with Jack, the more Ian looked like an angel. Sure, he'd been ever so slightly hinting at the fact that he wanted to meet me in Colorado—just for a day or two—but for the most part, I'd blown him off. He'd also had his doctor friend call in a new prescription, which at the moment, I was strongly considering picking up.

"Hey, Amelie?" Jack said interrupting my thoughts.

I looked over at him.

"I took a peek at your writing and…it's really good."

"What. The. Fuck?" I hissed, slamming my phone down on my thigh.

He flinched. "What?"

"How could you do that?"

"You read my mother's letters…"

"Oh, so that's how it is? An eye for an eye? I thought you weren't mad about that."

"I'm wasn't. I'm not."

I threw up my hands. "It's like we're children all over again."

"Yeah." He smirked. At that moment, I wanted to kill him. "But I just have to know one thing…" he continued. "Am I the 'J' you refer to?"

"Fuck you," I said, swallowing hard.

Jack laughed and turned his attention to the road. "You keep saying that." He sighed. "I like you better when you actually do it."

By this point, a light rain had begun to fall and all I could think of was how badly I wanted out of that Jeep and away from him. I'd already made up my mind that I was going to get on the first plane out of Colorado. I just hadn't said as much yet. I looked over at Jack and then checked my phone once more. There was approximately one hour and thirty-six minutes until freedom.

～

"YOU SHOULD CONSIDER FREELANCING," JACK MENTIONED, breaking the silence. It had turned from light to pitch black outside, and the drizzle had morphed into a steady rainfall. I had tried dozing off, but I was too angry for anything more than a restless sleep, and so I eventually gave up. "If things don't work out at your job, I mean."

"I don't want to freelance."

He tried handing me a bottle of water, a peace offering. I shook my head and turned away. "I think you'd be great at it… you really should give some thought."

I didn't respond.

"I'm sorry for snooping, Amelie."

"I'm sorry for being surprised." I shot back, unable to help myself.

"You are very talented." He took a deep breath. "And I'm not just saying that because I'm in love with you either…"

And there it was. He'd just handed over one more reason to run.

～

17

JACK

THE GREATEST SINS ARE THE KIND
THAT'LL DO YOU IN.

I saw it in her eyes first. She was going to run. I'd forced her hand, and she was about to tap out. As we checked into the hotel, I considered what to do about it. Really, I only had two options. Let her go. Or teach her to stay. I decided on the latter.

"Are you hungry?" I asked on the way up to our room.

"Starving," she answered. Her thoughts seemed somewhere far off.

I left it at that. But once we were in the room, no longer able to contain my anger, I lit into her. "What are you thinking?"

"Huh?" She turned, taking her attention off the minibar.

This is when I saw the third option. It was one I hadn't considered. I decided to play dirty.

"About food?" I said, unpacking my suitcase. "What are you hungry for?"

She shrugged.

"Well, I was thinking that we should have a drink and then take the shuttle into town."

She cocked her head, bit her bottom lip, and then nodded

as though my suggestion had confirmed something she already believed. "I thought you didn't drink."

"Yeah, well, a wise person once told me that one wouldn't kill me."

Amelie smiled curtly and then her eyes fell to the floor. "Better watch out, it just might," she said her eyes meeting mine.

I smiled, thinking she had no idea how right she was.

I DID END UP STOPPING AT ONE DRINK. BUT AMELIE DIDN'T need to know that. As far as she was concerned, we'd gone the four rounds it took to wipe out the mini bar. Once satisfied with her level of inebriation, I called room service and ordered dinner in.

"I thought we were going into town," she pouted.

I crossed the room and putting some distance between us. Then I sat down in the armchair across from the bed where I knew she'd eventually spread out. "Why? When we can have so much more fun here?"

"We should do something crazy!" she slurred.

I raised my brow and then grinned. "Oh, we are"

"What's that?" she asked half playfully, half shy. I'd always loved that expression she made.

"Well, for one, I'm going to strip you down, and then we're going to shower. And by the time we're done, dinner will be here."

Her expression gave her confusion away. "And then what?"

"And then I'm going to take my time with you."

She frowned. "That doesn't sound very crazy."

I pursed my lips. "Oh, trust me. It will be."

AMELIE AND I SHOWERED TOGETHER, AND THEN, STILL dripping wet, slipped into bed under the covers to find warmth within each other. She was giddy, drunk. Childlike and happy. I wasn't yet ready to employ my plan of getting straight answers out of her. I was just about to make love to her when room service arrived with dinner. I stood, wrapped a towel around myself and then searched my pants pockets for my wallet, looking for the cash I needed for the tip. From the corner of my eye, I watched Amelie tear the sheet from the bed, wrap herself in it and beat me to the door.

"I got it," she slurred as she flung open the door. It's rude to keep them waiting—"

Her voice instantly trailed off, and I turned toward her to see why she'd suddenly gone silent.

It turned out that Amelie's fiancé and room service are not the same thing.

"Ian," I cleared my throat. And then I made my way over to the door and stepped between him and Amelie.

"What in the hell is going on here?" he shouted.

I turned to Amelie, giving her the chance to answer only to find that she'd turned as white as a ghost.

"Probably about what it looks like," I replied, nudging Amelie further back into the room with my hip.

"Jack—don't," she said, her voice barely audible.

I closed the door a little more so that it was only halfway open.

Ian raised his voice as he spoke. "I want answers, damn it!" He attempted to push on the door, but I held it in place. Amelie stood just behind it, her back against the wall. When I looked back at her, she had her face in her hands.

"Amelie! I deserve answers, don't you think! Amelie! Answer me!"

I opened the door ever so slightly to allow her the opportunity to speak for herself. She didn't look up, and I took that to mean she didn't want it.

Ian peered in, and as my eyes followed his gaze, I realized he was taking in the state of the room. The empty liquor bottles on the counter, clothes strewn about the floor. His face reddened, and I watched as his stance shifted.

"I think you need to go," I told him, calmly.

"Oh, so I see what this is," he spat banging his fist against the wall, just outside the door.

At this point, a few brave and curious folks began to open the doors to their room and peer out, some simply being nosey while others just wanted to know what the commotion was all about.

"There's nothing to see here," I informed a middle-aged man, three doors down.

"Like hell there isn't!" Ian shouted. "We're supposed to be getting married in ten days and here you've kidnapped my fiancée. You've gotten her drunk, and I'm sure you've done God knows what with her!"

"Amelie's no child," I said, my jaw set. "And if you want to know what we did... ask her."

"No," HE MUTTERED, PINCHING THE BRIDGE OF HIS NOSE. IAN sighed and from there, his voice only grew louder. "I don't suppose she is a kid...you're right. I thought you were a faggot when, in fact, you're just an asshole...and as for her, well, she's A DAMNED DRUNKEN WHORE, THAT'S WHAT SHE—"

I shut him up by clocking him with the best right hook I could muster, landing it directly beneath his chin, sending him to the ground immediately. I stared at him lying there, out cold. And I considered that I probably shouldn't have hit him. But he'd caught me off guard. For starters. Amelie hadn't told me she'd planned to marry him in a week in a half. Also, although I wasn't happy with her—I couldn't let him make gay people and the both of us look bad. I could take it—but guys like Ian liked to pick on people who didn't deserve it. And that's why he got hit.

"Jack!" Amelie huffed as she burst from the room and knelt at his side. "Oh, my God, Jack. Look what've you done."

"He'll be all right," I said, shaking my head.

And the truth was the bastard would be all right. Save for a slight concussion and busted jaw, that is.

As for me, I wound up in the slammer.

I EXITED THE COUNTY COURTHOUSE AFTER SPENDING THE night behind bars. I emerged damp and filthy—tired and hungry. As I stepped out into the early morning light, I took a deep breath, the first I realized I'd actually taken since being handcuffed and placed in the back of a squad car the night before. I attempted to search for a cab, only the summer sun proved to be too much, so much so that I had to shield my eyes. When they'd finally adjusted, I looked up and there she was, just across the street, leaning against my Jeep, arms folded. She was wearing a white sundress, her blonde hair braided across one shoulder. For a moment, my mind couldn't rationalize how something so angelic looking could be anything but. She met my eye and smiled, and for a moment, I wasn't sure if I wanted to kiss her—or kill her.

At the hearing just prior to my making bail, I'd been informed that I'd been officially charged with assault. I pled not guilty, made bail, and stepped out into the cool morning air. As I walked toward Amelie, I considered that they might need to adjust the charges once I was done with her.

"Hello, Jack," she quipped, attempting to keep her voice neutral.

I ignored her and scooted past, reaching around to open the driver's side door. She studied my face as I reached out, took the keys from her, climbed into the driver's seat, and turned the ignition. I closed the door and watched her watching me. I gave a slight nod, put the Jeep in gear, and drove off. I didn't look back.

I'd hardly driven six miles outside of town before my anger got the best of me, and I pulled over to catch my breath and steady my thoughts. It wasn't just my anger at Amelie that had reached its boiling point. It was also my anger at myself. I turned the Jeep around at sat there for a moment, unsure what to do. I was only actually sure of two things. One, I was running. Also, that I was tired of running.

One way or the other, I was determined to put this whole mess behind me. And I decided to start with her.

As I pulled up to the courthouse, there she was seated on the curb in the same place I'd left her. I watched as the broken sunlight passed through the oak trees and lit the side of her face. And it made me sick to think that I wanted to stay there watching like that. I knew she'd heard the Jeep pull up, but she refused to look at me. Without shutting the engine off, I got out and walked toward her.

When I got to where she was seated, I stood towering over her, blocking the sun. "Why didn't you tell me?" I demanded.

She looked away, down the block.

I shifted my stance. "Had you seriously planned on marrying him in ten fucking days?"

She refused me an answer.

I exhaled and then sat down beside her. For a long time, we sat that way watching the people go by, each of them in their own little world, oblivious to the fact that mine was breaking in two.

Eventually, I threw my head back and gazed up at the cloudless sky. "I should have known," I told her. "This is always your M.O. You have me—and you have him, whomever *him* happens to be at the moment—and this way, you don't really have to give yourself to anyone. You're a juggler, that way. You always have been. And the reason I'm drawn to that is because...I get it. I'm the same. The trouble is I don't want to be the same anymore. Two wrongs never did make a right. And I can't keep doing this, Amelie. Going around and around. You've always been a very good friend to me, and yet, somehow, we always managed to blur that line, and each and every time, and without fail, it ends up in disaster. I thought we could go on this trip and that it would bring us closer together." I sighed slightly and continued. She still refused to look at me. "I don't know what I thought, to tell you the truth. Maybe a part of me thought I could win. That I could make you see, maybe even that I could make you different. But I can't. And I realize now that not only can I not win, but we're not even playing the same game."

She met my eye. "I should have told you the whole truth, Jack and I'm sorry."

"I'm sure you are. But sometimes, Amelie, sorry isn't enough."

"I know," she said, and then she hesitated and paused for a long time before she finally spoke again. "But if you think you know the whole truth—you don't. And the thing is I'm not sure it even matters. In fact—I know it doesn't matter.

And yet every fiber of my being wants to tell you. You're my best friend, Jack. I'm a mess. And if I can't tell you, then I don't know who I can tell. I don't know what's going to happen when I walk away from here."

I looked at her sideways.

"I'm going to lose my job." She swallowed.

"You're an amazing photographer, Amelie. You can find another."

"Just let me finish, Jack—I need to get this out. Before I decide against it."

I waited.

She took a long, slow breath in and held it. With her exhale came the whole truth. She told me about Brazil. She told me about paying the girl for the photos and how once word got out, she'd be useless in the industry. She explained this was why she'd agreed to marry what's-his-name and had followed him down the rabbit hole. She told me she was afraid of ending up, not only with nothing—but alone with nothing.

When she had finished baring her soul, as she put it, I decided to temporarily forgive her—at least long enough to finish up the trip. I don't know why I suggested continuing on—with a road trip which, up to that point, had been nothing but ill-fated—other than the fact that she looked so down. Honestly, I was afraid of putting her on a plane and sending her back to a place where she likely had no job—and a man waiting in the wings to manipulate her some more. Maybe that was a part of it. Maybe it was because she'd finally opened up. And yet—it was that which she had left out that had ultimately threatened to do us in.

~

18

AMELIE

LIES. AND OTHER HALF-TRUTHS.

I felt terrible for essentially getting Jack arrested. I fully understood as I watched him being carted off that this was all my fault. I should have been honest with everyone involved—most importantly, with myself.

I didn't love Ian. In my own messed up way, sure, I cared for him. Probably, in the same way that he cared for me. Whatever it was, though—it certainly wasn't love.

It was somewhere either right before or right after I caused Jack to get arrested that I realized it wasn't going to work between us. Certainly not now, and likely, if I walked away again—not ever. I also realized that it would be best if we had the conversation sooner rather than later.

Being on the road, particularly when you're in the passenger seat, the endless landscape set out before you, with nowhere to be and nothing to do, well, it gives you a lot of time to think.

And think I did. First, I emailed Ian and I apologized. Interestingly enough, his tone had completely changed when I refused to bend to his will and travel home with him. Not only did he agree to drop the charges against Jack, but also, he suddenly became a lot more forgiving than perhaps either of us had thought possible. He'd said that while he didn't understand my behavior, he could at least forgive it. His explanation was that I'd simply had cold feet—which was completely understandable and that once he'd had a one-night stand of his own and had gotten it out of his system, he realized that I likely had done the same. He told me that he understood getting married in Hawaii wasn't what I wanted—that I both needed and deserved a big wedding in the city. This was when I realized that he clearly didn't know me at all. In addition, I knew my getting fired was inevitable—just as inevitable as our relationship coming to an end. Which is why I went above his head and requested a transfer—before he had the opportunity to set anything in motion.

Ironically, it was Jack's mother's letter that led me to question what another route might be. But it was Jack who taught me to play dirty in finding where the alternate route would take me. I knew he'd gotten me drunk so I wouldn't leave. Somewhere just outside the Arizona state line, he'd admitted as much. What I didn't know was why he thought a temporary solution was the fix to a permanent problem. But I didn't ask as we'd agreed to spend the remainder of the trip on good terms. Jack had suggested that we continue on, driving to Flagstaff and then onto The Grand Canyon where we would stay in the vicinity for a couple of days. We would take in Sedona and then travel back down through New Mexico, hitting up Santa Fe, before making our way back to Texas where he'd drop me at Dallas/Fort Worth International Airport so I could catch the flight I'd booked back to Boston. Once back in Boston, I would collect my things from the apartment that Ian and I shared and decide where to go from there. Whether it be back to Texas or somewhere else. The trouble was Jack didn't know that somewhere else already had a name nor that I'd already set the wheels in motion.

It was Jack who'd offered me the exact plan of action I'd need to get out of the 'Ian situation' still employed. He told me to be honest with the management over Ian's head and to request to change my employment to freelance status. He also suggested that I threaten to sue on the term of harassment and/or wrongful termination—if management didn't comply. What Jack hadn't realized then is that management might one up his little plan and likely make him regret having suggesting litigation altogether.

TELLURIDE WAS PARTICULARLY BEAUTIFUL. THERE WAS SO much to do and so many photographs to be taken that it didn't leave much time for the examination about what we'd do once we reached our final destination.

Jack had grown quiet. Less argumentative, more loving. Telluride will always be a magical place for me, not simply for its beauty and charm—but because it's where I fell back in love with Jack.

"Where do you want to go today?" he whispered quietly just after we'd finished making love. It was the kind of sex where you both check your ego and leave it out of it. The 'what this might mean.' 'What happens next?' 'Where do we go from here?' All of it. In those blissful moments, there were no unanswered questions—we were just two people with very basic desires. Nothing more, nothing less.

Sated, I placed my head on his chest, and as I listened to the drum of his heartbeat, I tried to time my breath to it.

"I asked you a question," he said nudging the top of my head with his chin. "I asked if you had any idea of where you might want to go?"

"Anywhere with you," I told him and he laughed.

"I meant is there anything on the agenda that we need to see before we head out?"

"We should stay another day. Why rush off?"

I couldn't see his face, but I'm fairly sure I felt him smile. He squeezed me tighter. "That's exactly what I'd hoped you'd say."

Later, after we'd had breakfast as we stood waiting for the valet to bring Jack's Jeep around, he squeezed my hand. "I could get used to this," he said, without meeting my eye.

I cocked my head. "I assume you aren't referring to the valet parking."

"Here, this place. The weather. The view. You." He met my gaze then.

"Yeah, it's really beautiful," I told him. And then I looked away.

"There's nothing quite like the beauty of the Colorado sky," I remarked, snapping another pic. Jack turned and he smiled then. I captured it on film. To this day, that remains one of my most treasured photographs. We were headed up Bridal Veil Falls. It was early in the day, not too hot and not too cool. Just right, which didn't often happen. Jack had asked me about what I wanted to do with the future, and I'd dodged the question like a champ.

"I don't know much about the future," I insisted. "Other than that it's promised to no one." He looked over at me furtively. "I know you know that better than anyone," I said, slightly out of breath. Ten steps later, I had to stop to let my breath catch up with me. Jack did the same. He never stopped first, but he always took advantage of my taking a break. "But you know what I love most about photography?"

I asked without giving time for a response. "It's the ability to capture the present moment. Because it's all we really have, you know."

"I do know," he said.

And we both left it at that.

THE FOLLOWING DAY, WE LEFT TELLURIDE AND HEADED TO Arizona. This was where the road trip started to get fun. We played games, the way we had on that first road trip, way back when. Somewhere just past the Four Corners, where Utah, Arizona, Colorado, and New Mexico intersect, I took out my phone and Googled 'games to play on car trips.'

I found a list titled 'the best questions to ask on a road trip.'

"How would you dispose of a dead body?" I asked Jack without telling him we were playing a game.

"That depends," he said, glancing my way.

"On?"

He grinned. "On how I killed them."

This led us to a whole other conversation on the best ways to murder someone. There's a lot you can understand about a person, I realized—once you've seen them at their worst.

"I get to ask the next question," Jack said.

We'd laughed so hard over the most inappropriate of subjects that my sides hurt. Each time I tried to recover, he'd tell me the next most inappropriate thing. Understanding someone's mind in that way is incredibly intimate, and I'd started to feel uncomfortable. So I took the wheel and handed him the phone. He scrolled through a few, frowning until he'd come to one he deemed perfect.

"If you could marry anyone in the world, who would it be?"

I shot him a sideways glance as though to ask if he were joking. His expression told me he wasn't. I inhaled and then let it out slowly. "I don't know. I've never really wanted to get married."

"Ever?"

I shook my head. "No."

I considered how much to reveal. The truth was I really didn't see marriage in my future. But it was more than that. Should I tell him that I didn't want children—that I had no intention of having a family, of ever settling down the way most people do? Because the thing was, I knew Jack and I knew he loved me enough to say that he would be ok with that—when, at the very same time, I knew he wanted to be a father more than anything. How could I dash the hopes and dreams that he held for his own future—simply because mine weren't the same? And inevitably, we'd come to a place, down the road, where he'd just resent me for it. More importantly, though, I knew myself. I knew that I could stand a lot of things—loss, grief, even hate. But resentment wasn't something I could stomach. I didn't have it in me. Especially not where Jack was concerned.

As I stared at the floorboard, he cleared his throat. "So your engagement to what's-his-name then…it was all a lie?"

I didn't look up. "I guess that's one way to put it…"

"Why didn't you tell me it was serious back at Thanksgiving? At the airport, when I asked you, you said he was a friend. You didn't tell me I was flying to Boston to witness a marriage proposal. In a sense, it was like being ambushed." He looked over at me then, and I met his gaze. "I don't think I ever told you that.

I swallowed. "I know. I wasn't certain he was going to

propose although a part of me suspected. In any case, I fucked up," I admitted. "And I'll always regret that."

He nodded just slightly and then remained quiet for a long while afterward. Finally, he exhaled. "Well, my answer would be you. It has always been you."

I held my breath. I wanted to remind him, not always. Except, I thought better of it. Then, unable to take the intensity of his stare, I looked away.

"Next question," he eventually spoke up, a little too jovially. I took the wheel once more, handed him my phone, and watched as he squinted trying to read from the screen. "What is the one thing you wanted when you were a kid that you didn't have?"

"A mother and father," I answered, without missing a beat.

Jack looked over at me. "Yeah, me too," he said, his voice low.

I smiled ever so slightly as he reached for my hand, took it in his, and squeezed. "It's good to know we agree on some things," he remarked, raising the pitch of his voice. Only, when I looked over at him, his eyes were on the road, and he didn't look happy at all.

19

JACK

WHAT ARE THE ODDS?

$\mathscr{P}$erhaps I'm stupid. Or maybe, I'm just slow, but The Grand Canyon was the first place during our trip together I'd realized that Amelie and I weren't going to get our happy ending. In a sense, I think I'd known it all along. But this was the first time I really felt it down in my bones.

We were sitting in the Jeep staring out at the low clouds that had filled the canyon. We'd driven all this way and there was nothing to see—but thick white clouds blocking the entire reason for our visit

"What are the odds?" Amelie asked, her tone conveying that she was clearly trying to cheer me up. "We go to the desert and it rains. We come to The Grand Canyon and it's filled with clouds. We have interesting luck…"

I liked it when she used the word 'we.' "Yes, our timing tends to be a bit off."

She looked at me, took a deep breath, and then shifted in her seat to face me. I watched as she folded her feet underneath her. "We could give the tourist's another show…"

"We could…" I replied.

Amelie swallowed. "There's something I need to tell you."

I wasn't in the mood. I turned my attention to the windshield and watched the raindrops spatter it, one by one. "I hate it when you say those words. It never turns out to be anything good."

"I know."

I refused to look at her.

"Jack?"

"Hm?" I muttered, still unable to look her way.

"I did what you said," she told me, before she took a deep breath and let it out. "I requested a transfer and I got it."

I could tell by her tone that this wasn't good news. Also, that it had nothing to do with me. And yet maybe everything.

"They're sending me to Australia."

I looked at her then. "Australia?"

She gulped. "Yes."

"Well, that's about as far as you could get." I huffed, once again, shifting away.

"Yes, I know. But it's an assignment I need to take."

"I'm sure it is…"

"It's not like I'll get another opportunity like this—"

"How long?" I demanded cutting her off.

"Eighteen months."

I shook my head. "No, I meant how long have you known?"

She considered the question for a moment before answering. "Since Telluride."

I pursed my lips. "Telluride was five hundred miles ago."

"I didn't—I don't want to ruin our trip."

"And yet."

"I wasn't expecting this, Jack," she said and her voice broke.

We sat in silence staring out opposite windows for several minutes.

"You could come with me."

"I can't," I told her.

"Why not?"

"Because after Australia, it would just be somewhere else."

"Would that be so bad?"

"Yes, Amelie. Yes, it would. I have plans here. I have a life here."

She sat quietly for a moment and then she uttered the words that would haunt me for longer than I cared to admit. "I understand. And I hope you will, too.

IT WOULD TAKE A LONG TIME BEFORE I WOULD COME TO TERMS with her leaving again. Eventually, I would understand. In the meantime, I just played pretend.

Thankfully, for a few perfect moments, the clouds parted and then cleared just well enough for us to get a look at the Grand Canyon—and snap a few photos in the process. Looking back, those photos would forever signify the magnitude of what it meant to wait something out.

Having gotten our fill of the expanse of the Canyon, Amelie requested that we head down to Sedona. Along the way, she and I both seemed to tread carefully, putting our best effort forward, tiptoeing around minefields at the expense of what really needed to be said. We kept things light.

We arrived in Sedona just before sunset, and instead of checking into our hotel, we decided to drive around as Amelie desperately wanted to find the perfect spot to take photos of the setting sun.

"I thought we were going to camp," she murmured, staring into her camera lens as she pointed it out the passenger side window. "You bought all of that stuff." She sighed, as she lowered her camera and glanced toward the back seat. "And we haven't even camped."

"Yeah," I said flatly, "I changed my mind."

She shook her head slowly, her eyes on my face, reading me. "What a waste," she said.

"You have no idea," I told her.

I waited for a response, but instead, I watched as she changed out her lens, climbed out of the car, trekked up the embankment, and shut me out.

~

Dear Jack,

I've stopped all medication. The doctors have said they couldn't give me a definite timeline of how long I've got, even with the medication—but I know it likely won't be long. Honestly, it never would've been long enough, anyhow. I haven't told your father I'm not taking my meds. He would be livid, and sometimes, in life, and I guess in my case in death, you have to do what's right for yourself even if it's not right for those you love.

I understand that your dad wants me to continue to fight this. And I understand why. But what I've done this past year and a half one could hardly call living. I'm a prisoner, trapped inside a very weak and frail body, and I simply refuse to go on like this. It's incredibly hard to explain—but the best I can come up with is one morning, the morning I decided I'd had enough, was the same morning I had an epiphany of sorts. I realized, in my current state, I'm too small for this life. There are so many things that I want to hang around and see—namely you—as you grow up, but I can't go on like this. I watch your little face as I suffer, and I know it isn't right. A boy should not have to watch his mother fade away into nothingness. A husband should not have to put his dreams aside to care for a frail and hopeless wife. You both deserve so much better—even if you're unwilling to admit it. I want to see you out there, outside playing baseball or hide-n-seek with your friends. Not in here as you are now, sitting beside your bedridden mother. It's not fair to you. And as for your father, he needs to find love again. Someone who's his equal. Because that's what he deserves.

Many will say my throwing in the towel was selfish and cowardly. But I can assure you, it is not. Giving up is the most unselfish thing I've done in all my life.

As time goes on, and you become a man, I hope that you will fight like hell for what you want. But if there comes a time, where doing so means giving more—or getting less than you deserve, then I hope you'll think of me. And I hope you'll understand.

Love,
Mom

I read her words as I waited for Amelie to get back to the car. She'd trekked further up a hill, and I could just barely make out the faint outline from where she was perched trying to get the shot, as she'd put it. By the time she'd finished up, and made her way back to the car, I was sobbing. Startled by my state, Amelie stopped halfway inside the door and paused for a moment before slowly climbing in. Once she'd closed the door, she adjusted herself in her seat and then placed her hand on mine. "I'm sorry, Jack." I looked over at her and then away. I don't even think she knew what she was apologizing for, but the words she chose seemed to be the only ones appropriate for the situation.

I gazed out the window and considered how breathtakingly beautiful Sedona was despite the fact that the world around me was falling apart as I knew it. I missed my father immensely, even though our relationship had often been complicated. Through my mother's words, I'd come to see him in a new light. And there's something about losing a person forever that paints a different image in your mind. Their lingering absence clarifies the future and puts the past into perspective. One you couldn't have known before.

In spite of the fact that it's hard for one to see beauty when one is in so much pain, I sensed that Sedona was a spiritual place. It seemed to me to be the kind of place one goes either to heal or to find themselves again—maybe a little bit of both. I realized then that whenever I thought back on this trip in the future, Sedona would be one of the places that would always stand out most for me. Of all the places that we had stopped along the way, it turned out to be one of my favorites, second only to Telluride. Aside from every-thing else that took place, the landscape there was like nothing I'd ever seen. The colors—the reds and the purples more vibrant than I could have imagined. Not to mention, in all of the photos I'd seen over the years—not a one of them had done justice to the actual thing.

I looked over at Amelie then and wondered about the photos she'd taken. As I studied her face, I could see that she had been watching me—trying to discern exactly what to say. I was grateful when she said nothing.

IN THE MIDDLE OF DINNER, MY PHONE RANG. IT WAS JANE, AND this happened to be the third time she had tried to reach me that day alone—and for some reason, instead of once again sending it to voicemail, I decided to take the call. I answered, placing the phone on mute as I exited the restaurant.

Once outside, I perched myself against a column and pressed the mute button to turn it off.

"Hey, Jane, what's up?"

I could hear the hesitancy in her, even before she spoke. "Jack."

"Hello?"

There was a short pause. "I'm here," she said, her voice muffled and underwater. It sounded as though she were underwater—somewhere far off. "Listen, I don't remember when you said you were going to be back in Austin…"

I don't know why I said what I said when I said it. I hadn't even fully thought the idea through myself—at the time, it was just an inkling I had—something I thought I might want to do. If nothing else—it seemed to be a short-term solution to what seemed to be a long-term problem. "Um…I'm not sure. I don't think I'm planning on coming back just right away."

"Really?" she asked her tone conveying surprise and something else.

I sighed, all of a sudden very anxious to end the call. "Yeah, I'm thinking about moving to Colorado for a bit."

"Oh," she said, her tone flat. I heard her inhale sharply and then let it out. "Well, in that case, I guess I shouldn't beat around the bush…" Her words came out all jumbled together, fast, as though she hadn't quite thought them through. "I'd wanted to tell you in person, but given the circumstances…well… I guess I should just say it… I'm pregnant, Jack."

∾

20

AMELIE

WOULD IT HAVE MATTERED?

I sat in that restaurant on our final night in Sedona half hoping that Jack would ask me to stay in the U.S. and half hoping he wouldn't. As I picked at my dinner, I was irritated that my feelings on the matter seemed to change from moment to moment.

When I found out about the transfer to Australia, admittedly, I was intrigued. It meant a change, and to be honest, I was both ready and in deep need of change. At the same time, it wasn't a matter of whether or not I loved Jack enough to stay. In my mind then, and especially later, it would become a matter of whether or not I loved him enough to go.

During our time together on the road, I came to understand that the two of us were in a holding pattern. Neither of us willing to give an inch—yet still wanting to go the whole mile. And the truth was that no matter how much I loved him, I knew we couldn't get from here to there. Not with the current state of things.

Still, a part of me liked to believe love could conquer all—

that we could make it work—no matter what. I wanted to believe that with a bit of time and space between us—even an entire ocean—that we would come to the conclusion that we couldn't live without each other. At the same time, I understood that what I wanted for the future and what Jack wanted seemed to be very different things. In addition, given the current state of my life, there was also the understanding that a huge part of me didn't even know what it was I wanted.

When Jack stepped out to take a phone call, and I picked over my salad, I took the opportunity to think about what it was I really wanted in life. Adventure and change. And I realized that if Jack could promise me those two things, then perhaps our ideals weren't too far off.

As I waited for him to return, I ran back and forth over the scenario in my head, of the two of us saying goodbye once again. And I questioned whether or not I could really go through with it.

In the end, I decided to let my fate, the fate of the both of us, lie in Jack's hands. I needed to find out exactly what he had in mind for the immediate future and sitting there in that crowded restaurant, I knew there were really only two ways it could go. If he said he wanted to travel, then I'd stay in the U.S. and try to make a go of the freelance idea that he'd tossed out and see if the two of us could make it work. If nothing else—at least for a little while. But if he said that he was ready to settle down, then I'd go to Australia—putting as much distance between conventionalism and myself as I possibly could. Enough that I could forget—or at least give it my best shot.

By the time Jack finally arrived back to the table, his dinner was lukewarm at best while my spirit was high. I was hopeful he'd choose me and a life together on the road. I watched him as he took his chair and scooted in. He looked up at me and then down at his food before pushing his plate away. I raised my brow. "Is everything ok?"

He looked up at me once again, and I watched as something that looked a lot like dismay passed across this face. He swallowed. "Yeah, I'm suddenly just not very hungry."

I pursed my lips. "You want to get out of here?"

"I've never wanted anything more."

THAT NIGHT, WHEN JACK AND I HAD SEX, IT WASN'T ANY KIND of normal sex—it was pure, uninhibited, and animalistic. Basically, we fucked. He didn't caress me or take his time—it especially wasn't sweet and slow the way it had been for most of the trip. It was hard and fast, raw and primal. He hadn't even given me time to close the door to our room before he'd begun removing my dress. I smirked and shrugged at a fellow hotel guest as she eyed me up and down before I kicked the door closed with one heel and let Jack undress me. "I'm going to miss you," he said. "Better get it all out of our system now..." There was urgency in his words and in his touch that I hadn't felt with him in a very long time.

"I know you're upset—" I began, but Jack placed his finger over my lips to silence me.

Then he pushed me backward on the bed, spread my legs, knelt between them, and buried his head into me. And in the process, he made me forget anything and everything I'd wanted to say.

THE FOLLOWING MORNING, I AWOKE TO FIND JACK PROPPED UP on one elbow, laying beside me, his head resting in his palm as he peered down at me.

"Morning," I said offering a slight smile. I shifted and winced a little in the process, my whole body was sore. It seemed to remember before my mind did. He slid one of his hands beneath the sheets and cupped my left breast.

I inhaled sharply. "You're going to have to give me a minute. I'm still sore from last night…"

"We don't have a lot of time," he replied, pursing his lips.

"About that," I started and then paused. Jack looked away. "I was thinking that maybe you're right. Maybe I could give the whole freelance thing a go."

He looked back at me intently. I'd caught him off guard. "You mean not go to Australia?"

I sat up in bed and turned to him. "No, I mean, yeah… well, I was thinking that we could travel a bit… you know, and see where we end up. You could make it work, right? I mean, you could take a break from running your business for a while. Right? You've said yourself you have capable staff."

Jack swallowed and the shook his head. "I can't."

My heart sank. "Oh," I told him before I stood and walked to the bathroom. He followed. I tried to close the door, but he rested his hand against the doorframe.

"It's not that I don't want to."

"I get it," I said, eyeing his hand. It was a silent request for him to move it, to go away and let me be.

"No, you don't."

I didn't respond, and instead, I turned my attention to his reflection in the mirror and watched as he ran his fingers through his hair. After several seconds, he spoke. "Jane is pregnant."

My eyes widened and my mouth went dry. I tried to say something, anything, but the words wouldn't come.

"I know," he whispered reaching for me. "I'm in shock, too."

We stayed that way for several minutes, staring at one another in the mirror before I found the words I'd wanted to say. "Well, I guess that's that, then."

Jack rubbed at his jaw and then he looked away. Seconds later, he reached for the door handle, gave me one last glance, and then he turned and closed the door behind him.

WE DROVE THE FIFTEEN HOURS IT TOOK TO GET FROM SEDONA to Dallas mostly in uncomfortable silence, both of us realizing that while there might have been things we'd wanted to say, we had passed the point of any of it making any difference. We arrived late, after midnight and checked into a hotel at the Dallas/Fort Worth International Airport where I was to catch my flight back to Boston the following morning. My plan was to shower and go straight to bed, which I did. But in the early morning hours, unable to sleep, I went down to the coffee shop in the lobby. As I sipped my coffee and browsed the Internet via my phone, out of nowhere a familiar voice interrupted my reverie.

"You just slipped out," Jack said.

I didn't look up.

He sat down. "I'm sorry, Amelie. I didn't plan for this…"

I met his gaze then, his eyes weary.

"Would it have mattered?" I asked, more harshly than I'd intended.

"What do you mean?" he asked the confusion apparent in his voice.

"I just need to know… if she weren't pregnant—would you have let me go?"

"But she is pregnant."

My jaw hardened. "I get that. But it wasn't what I asked you."

Jack stayed quiet for a long while, shifting his attention to something on the TV in the corner of the room before he spoke, this time without looking at me. "No, I suppose this time I would have found a way to make you stay."

~

21

JACK

ONE LONG GOODBYE.

I learned a lot on that road trip with her. But it wasn't until the last leg of our trip that I was ready to acknowledge the greatest lesson Amelie, and our time together taught me—which was namely that sometimes in life, things don't work out quite the way you might have planned. But that doesn't make the experience of having lived them any less beautiful.

This was what I was thinking sitting there in the hotel as Amelie boarded her flight. I thought about how badly I'd wanted it to work with her. I thought about how I'd always wanted it to work out for us. Yet it never had—and inevitably, no matter how hard the two of us had tried—we never could get it right. I realized then that sometimes love is like that. It's unpredictable at best—and tough to swallow at worst. Watching her go this time, however, flipped a switch within me. Suddenly, I wanted to do better—to be better. Suddenly, I realized I had no other choice but to embrace what was and make the best of it. And I realized then that every time she'd ever left, it had made me better. I thought back over all of those summers together and how each time I'd grown from the experience of having loved her. I smiled just a little as the realization sunk in that this time would be no different.

As I started my Jeep to head back to Austin, I took one last look at the hotel, and I flashed back to her expression right before she'd walked off toward her flight. I thought about the way her arms felt as she'd given me one last sleepy hug. I recalled the way she'd pulled away and how she'd squeezed me and uttered something to the effect of congratulating me on my impending arrival. That was that, I thought, as I watched her fade into the distance. Mostly, I remembered that, as she walked away, I noted two things. One, this time she hadn't looked back. And two, no matter how the two of us appeared to be ripping the Band-Aid off at that moment, I knew, because I knew us—that this was sure to be one long goodbye.

I DIDN'T HEAR FROM AMELIE AGAIN FOR A LITTLE MORE THAN two and a half weeks. I had news that I was dying to share, and although I'd called her twice, she hadn't yet returned my call. She did, however, send me an email.

To: Jack Harrison

From: Amelie Rose

Subject: I know I owe you a call...

Dear Jack,

I'm sorry I've missed you the past few times you rang.

Life has been hectic here.

I moved my things out of Ian's place the day after I got back. Most of my belongings, I ended up putting in short-term storage. Over the past two weeks, I've either sold or donated the majority of my stuff—the rest I repacked and shipped to my mother.

The few belongings I have left (which, believe it or not, fit into just two suitcases) are here with me where I'm staying at a friend's house until I depart for Australia next week.

I'm actually beginning to get excited about moving to Australia. The dispersing of my things was surprisingly very cathartic, and I think I'm ready for a fresh start. It's always so interesting to simply be able to start anew—in a place where no one knows who you are—and where you can be whomever you want to be.

My mother spoke with one of my old docs, and by the time I arrived back in Boston, I had a prescription for a new medication to treat my depression and so far, so good. I've also found a psychologist here and she says that while it's too early to see significant changes, she's hopeful if I continue on this path—of therapy and the meds—that I'll see a dramatic improvement. Hell, I think just dropping the one hundred and seventy pounds that was what's-his-name was a dramatic improvement in and of itself. :)

Anyway, I'd better run for now.

But first, tell me what's going on your way...

Amelie

~

To: Amelie Rose
From: Jack Harrison
Subject: RE: You still owe me...

Dear Amelie,

That sounds great. You sound well.

As for me, I am adjusting to my new normal. Jane and her daughter have moved in here, and she's put her place up for sale. She's been pretty sick with the pregnancy, so I've taken leave from work in order to care for Molly. I don't know how much I've told you—but Molly is Jane's daughter. She is six and she's quite amazing. We've developed a little bond, the two of us.

Jane underwent some early testing last week, due to her age, and we'll get the results next week. I had no idea that it was even possible to be this anxious—but it is. They say the tests will determine the baby's sex, and to tell the truth, I'm not sure I'm ready to know. It's as though somehow it will make this whole situation seem more real and less like a dream.

AND that isn't even the news I was calling about… I wanted to hear your voice when I shared the news, but I understand moving halfway across the world is a full-time gig in and of itself, and so I'll just write it. We are moving to Colorado, close to Telluride. I loved it so much when we visited that I did a bit of research and really gave some consideration as to what I wanted next in life—other than being a father. In a sense, I guess, the realization that I'm bringing a child into this world has made me question a lot of things. And as for what's next, you are NEVER in a million years going to guess… but I've decided to move to Colorado and open up my own version of Camp Hope.

With the money my father left me, combined with what I'll receive by selling off a portion of my business, I should make out ok. Also, Jane has a lot of expertise in the non-profit sector with her background in social work and all. But mostly, it's watching Molly that has made me realize there's such a need. Jane has done an amazing job at finding resources for her and I can see what a difference it has made. And I can't help but think… what if you and I'd had those same resources…

I mean, Camp Hope was great, but it wasn't what we really needed. The camp I intend to create will teach more than just sitting around talking about one's feelings….

I KNOW! I can hear you now saying… YOU'RE DOING WHAT? You don't even like kids.

And at one time, I would have agreed. But now that I'm about to be a dad, I figure this—in addition to caring for Molly—is the best way to get my feet wet.

Love,

Jack

AMELIE

PROMISE YOU'LL KEEP IN TOUCH...

To: Jack Harrison

From: Amelie Rose

Subject: Congratulations!

Dear Jack,

It was so great to hear your voice this morning. Your phone call came so out of the blue it caught me a bit off-guard. Speaking of blue... Wow, a boy. I just can't imagine! I'm SO happy for you, and I cannot wait to meet the little fella.

Also, I still can't believe that you're opening up a camp for grieving children. Hearing the details really made it come to life for me. I think what you're doing is beyond amazing, Jack. And you are right—never in a million years could I have imagined that would be something you'd do. But I'm so impressed that you are. It's a very noble thing to leave your mark on the world in that way. I mean, it's a legacy you're building more so than a camp. Just think about how many people's lives you'll touch...

I often think about what I'll leave behind. I'd like to believe there's something, some part of me in the photos I take, but I don't know... I'd be lying if I didn't ask myself whether or not that's enough—particularly in my weaker moments.

That said, all is going well here in Australia. Our summer in the U.S. is their winter so it's colder than all get out here. The cold and dreary days make me question whether or not coming here was the right thing to do. Sometimes, I just miss home so much, you know? It's almost like the bleakness, the grayness of each winter day is there to remind me of how I feel.

My new therapist here assures me there's an adjustment period and while I understand that she's right, it doesn't necessarily make it any easier. To make matters worse, I don't know another soul in this country, other than the few people I've met in the office. People, I might add, in which I seem to have absolutely nothing in common with.

Anyway, I know it will get better. Until that time, I plan to throw myself into my work.

Lastly, promise me you'll keep in touch. I hope you'll let me do a feature on the camp once you're open for business. Also, I'd love to pitch the idea for an article and provide the photos for the feature. It would be a great excuse to come and see the baby.

Amelie

∽

To: Amelie Rose
From: Jack Harrison
Subject: RE: Congratulations!

Dear Amelie,
Thank you. Yes, I'm quite excited to have a son. And I will say that knowing he's coming has, in some ways lessened the grief I feel about my father's death. Not completely, but it does give me hope for the future in a way that I didn't know before.

I'm very sorry to hear that you're having a tough time. But I know you, and I know you'll rally rather quickly. You always have.
Also, I don't know if this is helpful or not, but I thought I'd share one of my mother's letters.

Perhaps there's some wisdom that will provide a bit of perspective… so I've scanned and attached it.

Must run for now. I have to get Molly off to ballet. Ballet. Ha! There's something I bet you'd never thought you'd hear me say. :)

Love,

Jack

Dear Jack,

This afternoon I watched your father teach you to ride a bicycle sans training wheels. As I studied the two of you together, it took all I had to bite my tongue and let you be. You're so alike, the two of you, in many ways. And yet, in others, you're completely different. I watched your little face, defeated and ready to give up, and I watched as your dad pushed and pushed you, refusing to let you give up.

There were so many times between attempt number one and number nineteen that I wanted to step in and save you. I wanted to tell you that it was ok—and I wanted to tell your father that you had plenty of time to learn to ride a bike and to ease up. But then there was the part of me that knew I wouldn't be around to see you grow up, and that there will be so many occasions much like this one in which I will not be there to step in. And that part of me realized I had to learn to let the two of you work it out. I had to let you find your own voice—just the same as I'd had to learn to drown mine out.

By attempt number eighteen—I know this because your father counted—you had two skinned knees, a bruised elbow, and one deflated ego. And I could see it on your face—you were seconds away from giving up. Only your father assured you that with a few more tries, you would get it. He drilled it into you that if you quit now, you'd let the pavement win—that every other try would have been for nothing. Then I watched as your face twisted and your expression turned from mere frustration to full out determination, and sure enough, the very next try, you got it. You peddled faster and harder and you stayed upright. But the best part wasn't seeing you ride a bike. The best part was seeing your shoulder's rise, you stand a little taller, and nothing but pure satisfaction playing across your face. Later, as I helped you clean up your battle wounds, I told you how proud I was of you, and I asked you how it felt to be able to ride a bike. Your answer was pure gold. "Not as good as proving to Daddy that I could do it." I then told you, "No, son, the important part was proving to yourself you could do it."

You smiled at me then and wrapped your arms around my neck. I hugged you tightly and whispered in your ear, "You're not a quitter, Jack. And that is usually the difference between failing and succeeding."

Never forget that son—whether you get something in the first round or on the nineteenth. Sometimes you will come out battered and bruised and worse for the wear. But, ultimately, it's the fact that you were willing to try again that made all the difference.

Love you always,
Mom

JACK

READ BETWEEN THE LINES.

ONE YEAR LATER. AND THEN SOME.

To: Amelie Rose

From: Jack Harrison

Subject: You nailed it.

Dear Amelie,

I just want to thank you once again for coming out last month. I saw the feature on Camp Legacy this morning, and you did a great job of encompassing the overall mission. I truly can't thank you enough.

I'm so glad that you got the chance to come and meet Max. I tell you what—the little guy's still giving me a run for my money. This whole zero sleep thing is rough. But like most parents say, completely worth it. Or at least they assure me it will be one day. :)

Molly seems to be adjusting well to being a big sister—though I do wish I had more time to spend with her. With the new baby and the grand opening, well, I'm not sure who let me believe that having/doing it all was a good idea, but let's just say that my hands are tied. She does, however, love the Polaroid camera you gifted her and has taken some of the sweetest photos I've seen. Aside from yours, of course. :)

It was also good to meet what's-his-name number two. I have to begrudgingly admit that I kind of like this one. Well, at least you could do worse, anyway.

Mostly, though, it was just good to see you happy. And much to my dismay, I'm almost certain I detected the slightest hint of an Australian accent in your voice.

Still, don't ever forget where home is.

Love,
Jack

❧

To: Jack Harrison
From: Amelie Rose
Subject: On nailing it...

Dear Jack,

I meant every single word I wrote. I'm still just so in awe of what you've created there with the camp. I remember when we first visited the area. I recall feeling its magic then—but now I don't know...it just seems magnified somehow. It's so beautiful. I just hope I did it justice.

Max is just the cutest and Molly was darling. Jane was nice, too.

As for what's-his-name number two, well, he barely made it as far as the flight home before I'd had my fill. I can't put my finger on it, but there was something missing. Not to mention there was the fact that he bored me to tears. Of course, you liked him, though. Of course, you did. ;)

I'm going to be crazy busy over the next few months with work. I have a few exhibits coming up here, and I'm so excited to get back to the art of showing my work—outside of the magazine.

Also, I have a bit of other news... some of my poetry is being published along with my photos. Nothing major, but it's been kind of a nice side project.

Well, it's late here, and I'd better hit the hay. Do give baby Max a kiss for me and tell him to let his Papa get some sleep.

Amelie

~

To: Amelie Rose
From: Jack Harrison
Subject: Hello?

Dear Amelie,

Well, I guess you have officially gotten too famous for us little guys.

Where are you? How are you?

I miss you, and I've been dying to get my hands on your book—although I can't seem to find it anywhere. I could've sworn you mentioned that it was out last month...

I even told the kids about it and they were excited. But seeing that you haven't written me back, I still don't have it in my hands and thus you've created two very unhappy children.

You should be ashamed. With your big head and your fancy friends and all. Hope you haven't forgotten about those of us who knew you when...

Call me sometime. Hell, at this point, I'd even settle for an email. Maybe even a text.

I miss you.

Love,

Jack

P.S. Max says thank you for his birthday gift. He also wants you to know that being two is really hard. Especially for his Papa.

~

To: Jack Harrison

From: Amelie Rose

Subject: RE: Hello?

Dear Jack,

I'm so sorry to have left you hanging. Don't worry about the book. It's probably not something you would like, anyway. But since you told the kids, I'll have my assistant send you a copy. :)

How is Max already two? I just can't believe it. My gosh, time flies.

How is Molly? The photos you sent are amazing. She really does have talent, Jack.

And Jane? Is the postpartum stuff easing up? I mean surely, it's been two years. I know it's not my place but have you considered having her see someone? I say this not to interfere— it's just that it has helped me ineffably.

So much so, I'm happy to report that I've met someone important.

I'm in love, Jack. :) And he's just the most amazing guy.

I'm hoping to come over at Christmas to spend some time with my mom. She wants to meet him. I also hope that maybe we can swing by the camp while we're there. I'd love to see your little family.

Amelie

~

To: Amelie Rose
From: Jack Harrison
Subject: Thank God. You're alive.

Dear Amelie,

I still haven't received your book... but I know you're busy, so I went online and ordered it to be shipped from Australia—given that it isn't available here in the U.S.

The kids are good. I'm well. And as for Jane, she's still, just Jane. It's been tough on her since Max's birth. But, then again, it's hard to say. Because the truth is, we hardly knew each other when she got pregnant. She's just so quiet all of the time. Sometimes, I swear she goes days without speaking. I don't know quite what to make of it, but some of my married friends tell me this is pretty normal. She's a great mother, though—even as quiet and checked out as she is, I know she really loves her kids. And to be honest, what more could a guy ask for?

I'm glad to hear you've met someone.

I can't wait to meet him.

I miss you.

Love,
Jack

~

24

AMELIE

YOU ROLL WITH THE PUNCHES...

*C*hristmas came and went and as planned. My newish boyfriend and I hopped a plane bound for Texas where we spent five wonderful days with my mother. It was neat to show Oliver life in the States, as he'd never been. We spent most of our time over the holidays in Texas revisiting my old childhood haunts and reliving the past.

So when we arrived in Colorado for the second leg of our trip over New Year's, I recall already feeling nostalgic. In Colorado, Oliver, the newish boyfriend and I spent quite a bit of time at Camp Legacy with Jack and his family although we didn't stay onsite. Colorado is normally magical, but at Christmas, it's simply spectacular. Telluride is one of the most beautiful places I've ever visited in all of my travels. Oliver agreed. Being there made me long for home in a way that I hadn't in a long time.

Oliver and I had met on a shoot nine months prior where I'd taken to him immediately. For starters, he's a brilliant lighting guy, and for the most part, the two of us had been inseparable ever since. Quite frankly, he's nothing short of amazing. I'd never met a man quite like him. Well, except for maybe one...

Still, I don't think I'd ever known anyone as happy as Oliver. From the time he wakes to the time he goes to bed, he's just... full on happy. He has this childlike quality about him that you just don't find often. Not to mention, being with him is just plain fun. The best part of it all though was the way his qualities tended to rub off on me, and in being with him, I've done some of my best, most creative work.

Looking back on the New Year's trip to Colorado, I've racked my brain to find something that seemed out of the ordinary—but I can't quite say I have. I just remember being very, very happy. I remember having the time of my life.

Oliver, I would later understand, recalled it just a bit differently.

SHORTLY BEFORE VALENTINE'S DAY, NOT LONG AFTER OLIVER and I had settled into our newer, larger apartment in Melbourne, I received a missed call from Jack. We hadn't spoken much—if at all that I recalled, since shortly after Oliver and I had left Colorado when I'd called to thank him again for the visit.

Things had been so hectic on set. I was shooting an ad campaign, and I hadn't immediately returned his call. The following day, two more calls came in. On the third call, I had my assistant answer.

I can still remember the way her face looked when she handed me the phone. "It sounds urgent," she'd said and so I stepped outside to take the call.

"Jack?"

"Amelie—" His voice came out rushed as though he were

short of breath. "Look, I know you're busy, but I just need to speak with you for a quick second. I don't know who else to call…"

"Is everything ok?" I asked—which turned out to be a dumb question to which I'd already known the answer.

I heard a long sigh. "Jane left me. And she's taken the kids. To Maine! She's taken them all the way to fucking Maine—with no warning whatsoever."

"What? Why?"

"I caught her having an affair last week—I walked right in on them."

I inhaled sharply. "Oh, my God. Jack."

"But you know what? At first I was a little angry… sure. But then, once I'd cooled down, I told her that it didn't matter. I told her she could have her relationship—but that we needed to do what was best for the kids."

I didn't know how to respond. "Wow. I'm really sorry—"

"She just left, Amelie." I heard his voice crack. "And she took my whole world with her."

"Have you spoken to her?"

"No. Well… not really. Mainly, just to the kids."

"What—" My voice was interrupted as I heard my name being called over the loudspeaker. "Listen… Jack… I'm sorry, but I've gotta run. They get super pissed about breaks here because these shoots cost like ten grand a minute. But I promise I will call you back just a soon as I'm off set."

He exhaled.

"I'm sorry. But I know it will work out."

"I'm not so sure." He'd sighed and then we whispered our hurried goodbyes.

∼

"Come on," Oliver pleaded. "Get yourself ready. It's Valentine's Day, for God's sake. We have reservations."

"Just one more second," I called distractedly from the couch as I propped my legs up on the coffee table.

At least five minutes or so later, I felt him standing over me. "Get. Off. The. Computer. Amelie," he demanded, as he pulled on my big toe.

As I glanced up at the man towering over me, I noticed while I'd been lost in my computer, he'd already showered and dressed. Meanwhile, I was still in sweats. He looked nice, his blond hair freshly cut just below his ear. One of my favorite spots to nibble. "I'm sorry," I told him as I motioned toward my appearance. I checked the time on my computer. "We're going to lose the reservation, aren't we?"

"If you don't tell your friend that you have to go—no doubt we will miss dinner," he said his Australian accent thick. "Tell him that you have a life here."

I turned my attention back to my computer. "All right," I huffed. "I'm logging off."

"You can't keep doing this, Amelie," he said, leaning against the bar.

I stood and placed my laptop on the coffee table. "I know —" I called over my shoulder as I made my way back to the bedroom. "It's just that he's having such a hard time… He's so down. His wife left him, Oliver. I mean—what am I supposed to do? He has no one."

He followed me into the bedroom, watching intently as I shed my sweats. I recognized that look, and knowing Oliver, I wondered whether or not we'd make it to dinner no matter how fast I rushed to get ready. "I thought they weren't married," he remarked, his eyes lingering.

"Well, not technically," I told him, waving my hand in the air. "But I mean… they've been together forever."

"That isn't the same thing as being married."

I cocked my head and raised one eyebrow. "Why not?"

Oliver shook his head slowly. "There's no commitment there."

I studied his face. "They have a child together. And he's practically raised her daughter. I'd say that's a pretty big commitment."

"Ok."

"Ok? That's all you've got?"

He shrugged, his bottom lip jutted out. "It's just—I don't see why we're spending time talking about them, that's all. When we should be talking about us," he said, smiling just a little then.

"Jack is my friend, Oliver. My oldest friend," I replied, slipping my dress over my head. I smoothed it out and then turned to him. "Is this ok? Dressy enough?"

He eyed me from head to toe. "It's perfect," he whispered, moving closer until we were standing eye to eye.

I looked away, in search of my nude pumps, and then back at him. "I just can't believe she left him like that. He's devastated…"

"I thought we were talking about us," Oliver said, shushing me as he moved his hands over my body, slipping one underneath my dress.

I exhaled slowly. "You're right," I agreed. My breath caught as he trailed his fingers along my inner thigh.

"It's simple," he indicated, stopping suddenly. "They weren't happy. I saw it plainly at Christmas. I didn't know them—so I thought perhaps that was just their normal, but for sure, you could see they weren't in love. At least not with each other. It sucks for the kids, yes—but it is what it is, Amelie. That's life. You—how do you American's say it? You roll with the punches." Oliver forced a smiled and then exhaled. Now—let it go and focus on what's right in front of you."

I frowned. "I thought they looked fine."

"You look fine," he whispered before he lowered me backward onto the bed where we slowly but surely forgot about our dinner reservation, making love instead. I recall it being nice. But my mind wasn't there. And I think he knew it.

25

JACK

UNANSWERED QUESTIONS...

To: Amelie Rose

From: Jack Harrison

Subject: The letter I'll never send...

Dear Amelie,

I finally had a chance to read your book. And while I have many questions...

The most important would be—why didn't you ever tell me how you felt back then?

I know the short answer is likely timing. Also, Jane—and the fact that she was pregnant.

Still, I can't help but wonder whether the two of us gave up too easily.

I know timing is important... and yet that doesn't make me love you any less.

I still hold out hope that someday soon we'll get it right.

Love,

Jack

P.S. I hadn't ever seen the photos you'd taken of our trip—not until the book, anyway. They are beautiful. But the poetry, man, the poetry... It just about did me in.

J typed that email and stuck it in my drafts folder. While I'd wanted to send it, things between Amelie and I are almost too good to ruin. For starters, she just so happens to be my only real friend right now. I'm not sure I could afford to lose that. Sure, there are others—though not many who aren't on my payroll—in one way or another. In addition, she's in a relationship with the Australian version of Zeus—who, try as I might, I didn't even completely end up hating. Also, there's the fact that she's really, really happy.

To: Jack Harrison

From: Oliver Kelly

Subject: Amelie

Dear Jack,

I hope you'll forgive me for reaching out this way. I got your email address from Amelie's phone. I'm also sort of hoping you won't mention that I reached out to you. Although I do realize that is completely in your hands and I will make do either way.

Moreover—I'm writing to request that you back off. I've never done this sort of thing before, and honestly, it goes against my nature, being a man and all.

Lately, however, Amelie has changed. She's gone from creative and lively to barely able to leave the house for fear of missing a communication from you. She worries, I know she does, about you. She worries that you have no one and she seems to feel great responsibility toward seeing to it that you're ok.

I sympathize with your predicament, mate, I really do. I accept that you come as part of the deal with Amelie, given the length of your friendship. But what I don't accept is seeing her happiness shift so suddenly. You have to know that leaning on her the way you are isn't healthy. She's happy, she's in a relationship with a man who treats her heart as his own, and she's at the top of her game career-wise.

I understand that you aren't. But what I don't understand is why you seem hell-bent on bringing her down to your level.

So, man-to-man, I want to request that you please back off.

Take care, mate,

Oliver

I read his email over and over, and if I hadn't hated 'Zeus-y boy' before—I certainly did now. And while I didn't respond, mainly because he didn't deserve a response, I also wasn't so impractical as to see that he wasn't entirely wrong.

A FEW DAYS LATER, I TYPED UP MY FINAL LETTER TO AMELIE— albeit another one that I would never send. I'd come to the conclusion that Golden Boy was right. I needed to move on. And while I wasn't going to outright say as much to Amelie, I wanted to put it in writing so that I'd have a reminder for myself every time I felt the urge to reach out.

The writing was on the wall. She was happy, not to mention, on the other side of the world, and I realized that it was in everyone's best interest if I pulled away.

It was past time that I let her be.

To: Amelie Rose

From: Jack Harrison

Subject: The last letter that I'll never send…

Dear Amelie,

How ironic is it that I'm writing a letter I'll never send?

Part of me feels ridiculous. But the other part realizes this is something we teach the kids here at camp (to write it out) and I figured, ah, what the hell? It can't hurt to get my feelings down on the page…

It was right around Valentine's Day when I read your book. It had arrived sometime during the holidays, but the office staff must have set it aside with all of the other gifts, mail, and donations we receive during that time of year. So, it sat there in the camp office for several months. I guess it was meant to be, though, because I just so happened to find it at a time when I really needed it.

Also, I guess I can kind of see why you were always so evasive whenever I brought up my interest in purchasing a copy.

It's funny to me how we can often tell the world our feelings and yet not the person to whom those feelings are directed. And that is in part why I'm writing a letter I'll never send. You and I have always been experts at never saying what needed saying. We've been experts at being evasive and blaming poor timing—instead of taking personal responsibility for the reasons we haven't worked out.

And while I understand this is not as black and white as I'm making it out to be—it still bothers me that I have left so many things unsaid. Of all the people on this planet, you would think that I should know how fleeting life and the people you love can be.

In lieu of that sentiment, I'm just going to say it:
I read your book of poetry and I realize how much of it is about the two of us. And while I wish you had shared those sentiments directly with me, I understand why you couldn't. Even if I'm angry about it. You see, there is nothing like the bitter taste of missed opportunity.

Speaking of which, I often think back on that day, right after my father died, when I left you alone in my apartment drunk, and I went to see Jane. What you don't know about that day is that I turned back twice. I wanted to start over, and at the same time, I wanted to fight. Mostly, I didn't understand how it was possible to both love and hate a person that much, especially simultaneously. The second time, I made it as a far as my front door. Only, I couldn't make myself turn the handle. So, I turned around, and I went to Jane's and I sought comfort there, where it was easy.

Looking back, we're fairly sure this is the day Jane and I conceived Max. And while I love my son dearly, and I do not regret him for a second, and above all, I understand that things happen for a reason, there will always be the part of me that wonders what might have happened if it'd been you I sought comfort in.

And although it wasn't, it doesn't change the fact that I loved you then like I love you now. As time goes on, and as life changes, I know that I have always loved you, and a part of me always will.

But that love also has a flip side. It has a dark side, and it's one that I'm not particularly proud of… That love has cost me—it has cost more than I would like. You see, Amelie, loving you has caused me to hold on—when I should have been letting go. Holding on cost me my first marriage. It cost me my relationship with Jane—and ultimately, it cost me having my children nearby. And while Jane and I, despite the dissolution of our relationship, are doing our best to do what's right for the children. The bottom line is that I hurt her. Worse, the truth is I was never really in love with her to begin with. Which brings me around to at least half of my point. I hope that you'll forgive me if this isn't making sense. I'm clearly not as good a writer as you are.

That said, the point is this—aside from my various businesses, Camp Legacy, and being a father, there is nothing else I have ever put my whole heart into—because a part of it has always remained with you. This isn't your fault, as much as I'd like to blame you, and as easy as a copout as that would be. The truth is that's what I've always done—and it's in part why I haven't moved on.

Only that has to stop—I realize that none of this is your fault. It's mine. And I've come to understand I have to let go. I realize I can't very well teach the children who show up to the camp that I've built about moving on—if I've never been able to do the same. I am a hypocrite, Amelie, and in the worst way.

I am in love with someone who might never love me back in the same way that I love her. I am in love with the idea of you—and not what actually is. Perhaps this is how it's always been.

With that said, enough is enough. But first, true to form, I will give this one last-ditch effort.

I will tell you that I love you—that I've always loved you. Because that's what I've always wanted from you. And if I can't have it, then I can at least offer it myself.

I want you to know that you are my very best friend and, more often than not, you are the first person to cross my mind when I wake in the morning and the last person I think of as I drift off to sleep. I want you to know that whenever something happens in my life—good or bad—you remain, after all these years, the first person I want to tell.

So, while I'd like to believe that there's hope for a man like me to find love again—if it's not a love like that, then I don't know what hope it has.

If one can love another this much and yet still cannot make them stay—then, tell me, what are the odds for love at all?

I don't yet have the answers to these questions. But I do know that I have to find them. I'm too stubborn to go about it any other way.

So, with that, here's one final request—if there's even one tiny, minuscule part of you that wonders the same, I hope I'm the first person to know.

Love,

Jack

26

AMELIE

TIMING IS EVERYTHING.

$\mathcal{T}$he email came in on a random Tuesday. To say that it came out of left field would be an understatement. I read it quickly and then read it again just to make sure I was seeing what my mind believed it had just read. Admittedly, at first it shocked me, and then it pissed me off. I typed Jack's name into my email and let my fingers do the talking.

To: Jack Harrison

From: Amelie Rose

Subject: What in the hell…

Jack,

What in the hell…

Am I supposed to do with this?

Amelie

He responded right away.

To: Amelie Rose

From: Jack Harrison

Subject: What do you mean?

Dear Amelie,

What a surprise…hearing from you.

Also, I have no idea what you're talking about?

Enlighten me.

Jack

I read over his email and flung myself backward in the chair in my living room. Seriously? That's how he's going to play this?

To: Jack Harrison

From: Amelie Rose

Subject: Your sense of timing.

Jack,

Seriously? You're going to make me spell it out?

Well, all right then…

Why are you letting me in on your feelings now?

After all of this time?

I don't understand.

Amelie

Jack didn't write back for nine hours. I'd gone to bed, but sometime around three in the morning, I awoke, in full sweat. Once I'd gotten up, caught my breath, and recovered a little—I grabbed my phone and checked my email.

To: Amelie Rose
From: Jack Harrison
Subject: I don't know what else to say…

Dear Amelie,

I don't know what else to say…

Other than, I'm sorry.

I'm not sure where to start… but here it goes and at this point, anything other than honesty is a waste.

I wrote the email you received four months ago… and I'd never intended to send it. Only— I'm an idiot.

And true to form—I let Max play on my phone. As a token of his appreciation, Max somehow sent out everything that had been sitting in my draft folder. I guess one should have considered that entrusting a three-year-old with something important wouldn't lead anywhere good.

And yet—here we are.

Basically, back when I wrote it, I just wanted you to know how I felt. Given your recent engagement (by the way, how many does this make now?) I understand that it couldn't come at a worse time.

For that—I'm sorry. I also apologize for Max. For his chubby little fingers—for him sticking them where he shouldn't. In some ways, though I think he's smarter than his old man is. And that I won't apologize for. I also won't apologize for my feelings. They haven't changed. Not in several decades—and certainly not in the last four months.

As for what you're supposed to do with them… well, I'll leave that up to you.

Love,
Jack

~

FOR THREE WEEKS, I WALKED AROUND IN A DAZE. JACK'S EMAIL had thrown me. Suddenly, I found myself quite unexpectedly questioning things that had happened years, even decades ago. Now, I was questioning everything about the current reality of my life.

To make matters worse, Oliver was shooting on location in the UK—which meant he wasn't home to settle me as he so often did. After receiving Jack's email, I called in sick and lay in bed for two days straight after Jack's last email. I hadn't responded to him, and to tell the truth, I wasn't sure I planned to. What I also hadn't planned to do was to get married. But Jack didn't need to know this. Not now—and maybe not ever. The truth was Oliver and I never intended to actually get married. He simply liked the idea of calling me his fiancée versus his girlfriend. To him, it implied a greater commitment. To me—it didn't matter one way or the other. I was happy with the way things were. Or so I thought.

Only without being able to discuss my newfound problem with the one person who would understand, I resorted to the only one who had known me longer.

"Mom?"

"Amelie?"

"Hey…" I sighed heavily.

"Is everything ok? It's early there."

"Yeah, I'm fine."

I listened as she audibly exhaled.

And then her voice raised several octaves. "Oh, I've been meaning to ask you…did Oliver get the gardening books I sent?"

"Um, I think so—" I said. "Listen… Mom, I need to talk to you about something."

I could practically see her there in her kitchen, which was where she always took her calls, as she braced herself. "Ok?"

I inhaled sharply. "Jack is in love with me."

"Jack has always been in love with you, dear."

"But this is different. I mean this time—he…" I tried to go on, but for the life of me couldn't find the right words.

There was a long pause. "Amelie. I'm not sure I'm following… maybe you just need to get some sleep, sweetheart. You sound tired."

"I'm not tired… well, I am tired—but that's not the point. I just don't know what to do."

"What to do about what?"

I felt my cheeks grow hot. "Have you not been listening this entire time?" I screeched into the phone. "I'M TALKING ABOUT WHAT TO DO ABOUT JACK?'

Her voice remained calm. "But you just got engaged to Oliver, honey."

I sighed again, exasperated. "That's my point!"

"You do love him, don't you?"

I pinched the bridge of my nose and squeezed my eyes shut. "Of course, I do. It's just that—"

There was another long pause. And then my mother spoke softly, carefully, "Look, honey, I know that Oliver is away and you're probably missing... him, but I really think you just need to get some sleep. Engagements can be tough. It's a change. Change has always been a bit unsettling for you."

"We're not getting married, Mom."

"What do you mean?"

"I mean—that the two of us have no intention of ever tying the knot. Oliver knew that when he popped the question."

"Oh," she said, clearly taken aback. "Well, he obviously loves you."

"Yes—" I answered my tone flat. "But he also seems to be well aware that I'm in love with someone else. I'm afraid that maybe he knows me better than I know myself..."

"What are you saying, Amelie?" Her voice had grown colder.

"I'm saying that I don't think there's anything that I've ever put my whole self into. Nothing. Not one thing—"

"That's not true. What about your work?"

"Maybe," I told her. "But lately, I've begun to wonder whether or not that's enough."

THREE WEEKS LATER, I WAS SITTING ON A BENCH IN THE PARK. I'd just finished a shoot. It was a magazine shoot—and not the one I'd come to Australia for. Thanks to Jack's freelance idea, I'd renegotiated my contract, which allowed for much more flexibility in jobs I was able to take on outside of the travel world. Initially, I enjoyed the freedom it provided. But lately, the gigs all seemed to be the same—just another up and coming twenty-something-year-old star who was to be featured in a major publication whose photos would be so retouched it mattered not whether my work was any good at all. I figured, in the end, neither the photos nor the subject ever resembled the original anyhow.

This is what I was contemplating when the little girl suddenly caught my eye. She was young—maybe four, or so, and as I watched her, I noticed her mother watching me. The little girl rounded the playground once more. She'd been running in circles, chasing after a little boy, her long blonde hair swaying behind her, struggling to keep up. On the third round, she stopped just shy of the bench and stared at me intently, her hands on her hips.

"What's your name, lady?" she demanded, panting. Up close, I couldn't help but think she looked at lot like me at that age.

I cocked my head to the side and cleared my throat. "I'm Amelie."

She looked around, whipping her hair around her. "Where's your kid?"

My hand flew to my throat, and suddenly, I felt her mother's eyes on me. "Oh—I—I don't have any kids?" I said, with a slight shake of my head.

She jutted one hip out and furrowed her brow. "Why not?" she asked with conviction, as though it were the most logical question in the world.

"Um…well, not everyone has kids."

"But you're old."

I snorted. She'd caught me off guard. Then I laughed. "And you're quite cute," I told her.

"Evie," her mother called after her rather sternly. I watched as she crossed the playground, reaching the bench in three short strides. She placed her hand on her daughter's shoulder and didn't meet my eye. Evie must look like her father, I considered as I studied the woman's face. She crossed her arms, still looking down at the little girl. "What did I tell you about talking to strangers?"

Evie's face fell. But she recovered quickly. "She's Amelie. She's not a stranger and she doesn't have any kids…"

The woman didn't say anything. She looked at me briefly before looking away as though she were searching for a way out.

"No, not yet I don't," I told the little girl with a smile. "But if I ever do. I hope she's exactly like you."

Her face lit up and it changed my life forever.

OLIVER ARRIVED HOME ON A SATURDAY AFTERNOON. HE WAS jet-lagged so I went for a hike and ran a few errands, but we'd agreed to meet for dinner later that evening at a small cafe not far from our apartment. He was waiting at the restaurant when I arrived. As I watched him sitting there at the table, looking off into the distance, something in me sank, and suddenly, I felt deflated. He made me happy, and I realized then just how much I'd missed him.

Oliver looked up then, and I made my way over to the table and took my seat. He stood to kiss my cheek. "I'm starving and you're late," he said as he scooted his chair forward.

I checked the time on my phone and frowned. "Just by a few minutes—I'm sorry."

"Minutes, even seconds can be the difference between life and death, you know," he remarked, his accent thick.

I leaned back in my chair and shifted a bit.

After several minutes of silence, he waved me off. "No, I'm the one who's sorry," he said running his hand through his blond hair. "I'm just tired."

I pursed my lips. "Yeah, me too." I leaned in studying his expression. "So—tell me, how was your trip?"

I listened as he rattled off words I didn't hear, my thoughts still on the little girl in the park.

"Amelie?"

He got my attention then. "Oh—sorry."

"Where'd you go?"

"Huh?"

He raised his brow, his eyes bugging out a little. "Just then, where'd you go?"

"Oh," I smiled as I brushed my hair out of my eyes. "I was just thinking…"

"I ordered for you. Your usual."

I nodded slowly and watched as he sipped his water. "I was thinking I want to have a baby…"

Oliver choked. I handed him his napkin.

He dabbed at the water dripping from his chin. "Amelie. Jesus."

"I was thinking that the baby should have my eyes and your wavy hair. And—even if it doesn't—that's ok." I paused and grinned. "I'm sure we could find a way to love it anyway."

He glanced around the cafe and then back at me. "Are you joking?"

I frowned. "No. Not at all."

"But—we discussed this. We don't want children."

I swallowed. "I know—I didn't. But that was before… I'm

getting older and well, I was in the park... and I saw this little girl and—

He cut me off. "You saw a little girl and what?"

"And I changed my mind..."

"You can't just go back on your word, Amelie. We had an agreement. I don't want children."

I felt my face grow hot. "Well, I'm not sure I agree anymore."

"What about your career? What about mine? Children aren't toys, Amelie. You can't just drag them along anywhere you want. Children are a huge commitment. And not one I want."

"I—I was thinking that I could take a few years off. And I know they aren't toys, Oliver. But I don't want to miss out either—"

"It sounds like you've really thought this through."

"I have. Sort of."

"Sort of?" He huffed. "That's typical."

Then he stood suddenly and placed his napkin on the table.

"Where are you going?" I asked, watching his face. He opened his wallet and tossed a few bills onto the table.

"All of a sudden, I'm not hungry anymore."

I watched as he walked out of the restaurant without looking back. And that was that.

～

27

JACK

THE TEST OF TIME...

*I*t was a random Thursday when I was called over the two-way radio to the office to sign for a package. Max had just left to go back to Maine after visiting for two weeks, and I'd taken to hiding my devastation at his departure by rebuilding a fence. Annoyed that I'd have to ride all the way back to the office, I asked that the mail carrier bring the package out to me. I knew that I was being absurd, but I was too angry about Max going back to Maine with his mother and new stepfather to care. I heard some debate over the radio and then it went silent.

I went back to my fence building and paid little attention when I heard the mule making its way toward me. Mostly, I was thinking about summer in Colorado and how lovely it was. Still, I couldn't shake the overall state of discontent that had become my life recently. I was contemplating leaving the camp, leaving Colorado—heading to Maine to be close to Max. This was also not boding well for my mood.

"Hey, cowboy."

My back stiffened at the sound of the familiar voice. It took a few seconds, but eventually, I turned.

And there she was. Dressed in cutoff shorts, wearing a smile as big as Texas.

I stared, unable to formulate words. She walked toward me. "I can't quite tell if you're happy to see me," she said as she threw her arms around my neck. "Cat got your tongue?'

When I pulled back, she was grinning.

"What are you doing here?" I asked, before leaning in again, squeezing her tight.

She shrugged. "I missed my oldest friend…"

I wiped the sweat from my brow and tried to gauge her expression. "He missed you, too."

"I'd forgotten how much I've always loved this place," Amelie declared, staring out the passenger side of the Jeep that I'd never been able to get rid of. Leaving the fence mending for another day, I'd cleaned up and showered, and Amelie and I decided to drive into Telluride for lunch.

"It could love you right back," I assured her.

She looked over at me and smiled and then turned her attention back to the clouds.

"This view." She sighed. "It's just so beautiful."

I looked over at her then, took her hand in mine, and smiled. "Even more so now."

When we were halfway through lunch, the restaurant mostly empty in the off-season, I finally asked her the question I'd been dying to know the answer to. Once I'd finished my burger, I cleared my throat. "So, when are you going to tell me why you're really here?"

She looked up at me, her expression serious. "I told you."

I just stared, watching as her expression turned playful.

"I missed you," she said.

"How long will you stay?" I asked my stomach in knots. I looked away as I braced myself for the answer.

"Oh, I don't know…" She sipped her water. "But I was thinking maybe as long as you'll have me."

My eyes met hers. "Are you serious?"

She swallowed. "Well, there is one condition…"

I eyed her intently. And I waited. She made me work for it.

"And?"

Amelie placed her glass on the table. "I want to have a baby."

I did a double take. And then I made her say it again. "You what?"

"I want to have a child, Jack. Of my own."

I studied my plate, picking at my fries. "Wow," I said as I popped one into my mouth. "That's certainly the second most unexpected thing I've heard all day."

"Only the second?" she teased. "What was the first?"

"Your voice."

She nodded.

I stuffed several fries into my mouth even though I was already full. "Well, I'll have to give it some thought," I told her, once I'd swallowed my mouthful.

"I'm sure."

I looked up at her then. "So, when you say you want to have a baby…you mean with yours truly?" I was giving her a hard time. I'd understood what she meant.

She shrugged, knowing me all too well.

"Why?"

"Well, you already have one and he's pretty cute… so I just figured… why not?"

"You're crazy," I told her.

"You're not the first person to tell me that." She laughed.

And I fell more in love than I'd ever been in my life.

Or so I thought.

~

LATER THAT EVENING, AFTER WE'D SPENT THE ENTIRE afternoon wrapped up in each other, I'd gotten up to call Max to tell him goodnight, the way I did every night at that time while Amelie napped in my bed. I stepped out onto the wrap-around porch I'd helped build with my own hands to make the call.

Once I ended my call with Max, I sat there watching as the sun drifted lower into the horizon. I considered for a moment how it was possible to be so incredibly happy and so sad at the same time. I realized as I watched the day fade away that no matter how happy I ever became, a piece of my heart would always be absent. The truth was I missed my son more than I could have ever imagined and hearing his little voice always drove the point home.

I heard the door open and watched as Amelie peered out. Spotting me, she stepped out, wrapping my bed sheet around her, and sat down in the chair next to me. I pulled it closer and turned my attention back to the horizon.

"It's beautiful out here…" she said.

I looked over at her and lingered. "Yes, it is," I whispered.

"Are you ok?" she asked, reading my mood.

I nodded. "I just got off the phone with Max," I replied, holding up the phone for good measure. "I miss him."

"I can see that," she said quietly. Then she repositioned herself to face me directly, propping her legs underneath her in the process. "You should consider moving to Maine…"

I didn't answer right away. "What would I do in Maine? The rest of my life is here." I watched as her face changed, her gaze fixed on mine. Eventually, I shrugged. "Plus, like you said, it's beautiful here."

"I'm sure it's beautiful there, too."

"Yeah…" I added as my eyes drifted to a piece of plywood in the floor. "But what about you? Would you move to Maine?"

Amelie reached over and grabbed my chin forcing me to look at her. "I'd go anywhere with you."

I pursed my lips, and I didn't take my eyes from hers.

"We could open another camp. In Maine. I could teach photography…"

My face lit up unexpectedly. "It sounds like you've really thought this through."

She smiled. "I have. It's why I'm here."

I scoffed. "To save me?"

She swallowed, jutted out her bottom lip, and then shrugged. "And to be saved right back…"

IN THE EARLY MORNING HOURS, AFTER WE'D MADE LOVE YET again, I held Amelie. Then I asked what had changed her mind. I interrogated her again on the reasons why she'd really come back to the States and more importantly, to Colorado. Mostly, I wanted to know how I could be sure this time she'd really stay.

She sighed and then she told me a story. "I've always loved you, Jack. You know that. But—when I read your letter, or rather your email, the one Max sent—it caught me off guard. I thought I was happy in Melbourne. I thought I was happy with Oliver. And for the most part, I was. Yet, there was this little part of me that still held the question. At first, it was tiny—but it started to grow. And then one day, I was in the park. To tell you the truth, I don't even know why I went there. I felt unsettled and so I was wandering the city, with no clear-cut direction, and when I found a bench, I just decided to sit. And before long, there was this little girl who appeared and she looked like me, which was really, really uncanny. It's hard to explain, but suddenly, the tiny question in the back of my mind that had been asking me if my life was enough—if I was sure that I didn't want children— suddenly, it began to scream. And for the first time, I considered that there might be another way. I realized that I'd never aside from my work here and there—ever put my whole self into anything. And I was tired of running. I was tired of trying and coming up short. So, I read your letter again. In fact, I read most of the emails you've sent me over the last several years...which were mostly about Max and...well, I realized that, yes—I do want to be a mother. But it was more than that, too. I realized that you have been the one constant in my life, and if I had my way, you likely always would be. Through everything—it's always been you. Just like your email said. And then I knew. I knew I wanted to be with you. All of a sudden, life in Australia—suddenly, a life so far away, became more than not enough. It became unbearable." Amelie drew a long breath and exhaled before continuing. "Only there was Oliver to consider. And I did love him. He was... he is a good man. At the same time, I realized that wasn't enough. And I knew the best way out of it was really the only way. I knew he'd never wanted kids..."

"And now?" I whispered into the dark.

"And now I realize that all of the false starts—all of it—all the fights—the heartbreak, the leaving—it was all just a test to see how much I really wanted the real thing. Obviously, I didn't want it badly enough then. But I do now. I guess you could say I grew up. I don't know how else to explain it..." Amelie turned and looked up at me. "If you're on board, I say we go to Maine... you can be with Max and fingers crossed—you and I can hopefully, finally, get it right."

"You sound pretty sure of yourself," I told her, half-jokingly—half-unsure of what to say.

Amelie buried her head into my chest and then pulled back. "I'm only sure of this," she said motioning between the two of us. "I'm sure of what's right here in front of me, willing to let me love him—if only I'll let him love me back. I'm sure that you've always been the person for me—even when it seemed like you weren't. I just had to grow up a little bit. Or a lot. And maybe you did, too. But mostly, I'm sure that I'm willing to fight for what I have here, in this moment. I'm willing to fight for the rest of our lives to never forget my path back to you. To never forget that it's always led me back—one-way or another. And I'm sure that I'm willing to fight to hang on to the memory of what we have—what we've always had. No matter how rough the road ahead might be."

"And what's that?" I asked, testing her. "What do we have?"

She smiled. "Chemistry. Love. Friendship. Hate-ship. Which if you ask me—is just another form of love," she said, and then she let out a small laugh. She paused for the briefest of seconds and exhaled. "It's something exceptional—that's what."

"I think you're exactly right," I told her.

"Of course, I am," she said without missing a beat.

And just like that, she'd passed the test. Then again, I knew she would. She always had.

～

EPILOGUE

JACK

Happily ever after's do exist. Sometimes, they just take a while.

Three weeks after Amelie arrived back in Colorado, we packed up and moved across the country to a tiny town in Maine. We road tripped it there in a U-Haul filled with only that which was a necessity. Letters, photos, and a bed. Two weeks after we set out, we sleepily pulled into that tiny town and turned down the long drive of a small rundown cottage that Amelie had her heart set on renovating from the moment she saw its photo online.

We spent the next six months turning it into our dream home—complete with a photography studio around back for her, a detached office for me, and a spare room for our future child. We were blissed out happy.

But the best part—aside from falling in love with her for new and different reasons than I ever had before, was being close to Max again. I was able to be a day-to-day father again versus simply a vacation dad.

There was also the factor of seeing Amelie with him. She

was a natural. More importantly, she never tried to play 'Mom' with Max. She was always a friend first, confidante second, and person of authority last. She let Jane and I handle the parenting side of things, and this is what I believe made our blended family situation work so well.

But this doesn't mean it was always easy. We had immediately begun trying for a baby. Essentially, starting from the day she arrived in Colorado. By the third month, Amelie began to worry that nothing was happening while I assured her it likely had to do with the timing and stress of moving to the east coast. By month six, just as soon as the renovations were complete, she seemed to go into full-blown panic mode. I chalked it up to the fact that we'd just spent the last half a year of our lives tied up in one project after another. And sooner, rather than later my nonchalance about the lack of conception drove a bit of a wedge between us. I insisted that if she were so worried about it, then she should see a doctor, a suggestion that she flat out refused. I had never, as long as I'd known her, ever seen Amelie so stressed out over something as much as she was about not getting pregnant. Amelie wasn't a worrier. She didn't fret over things. She wasn't a planner, and most of all she was an eternal optimist. Which are all reasons why I fell in love with her. Only, without anything to show for all of our practice (which was the fun part I might add) she became withdrawn and moody and different. She became depressed.

I did my best to love her through the darkness. But the truth was I wasn't very good at it. In addition, as she often pointed out, I already had a child. So I didn't—couldn't—and according to her, never would get it.

By month fourteen, Amelie finally agreed to see a doctor, who after several rounds of tests, found absolutely no reason for our infertility. She added that we could try the more modern scientific methods of conceiving or we could wait it out. I wanted to proceed with in vitro— while Amelie threw all of her energy into Eastern medicine.

Somewhere during our second year of trying, we both decided to proceed with our plans of opening Camp Legacy II. Initially, when we'd arrived in Maine, I wanted to hold off in order to get the house situated and to get settled. Mostly, I wanted to spend some time getting aquatinted to our new lives and to avoid another situation like what had happened when Max was born—where I was simultaneously becoming a father and an owner of a new business.

This remained the plan until one evening I arrived home to find Amelie in her studio, a sobbing mess on the floor, photos spread around her. She missed her job, she missed traveling, and she felt that she'd given it all up for nothing. Despite the fact that I was initially hurt by her sentiment, I couldn't say that I completely disagreed. I still had my work, for the most part. I was running all things for the Colorado camp, as well as my various business partnerships, and on the side, making plans for the new camp. As for Amelie, she took photos here and there—but mostly, she sat in her studio, day in and day out, thinking about everything she'd given up and all that she didn't have to show for it. She said she'd had enough. She was done trying for a baby, that it wasn't meant to be, and couldn't be forced.

While I didn't completely agree—I didn't tell her as much. Instead, I suggested the one thing I knew she needed more than anything. Adventure. So we agreed that we'd proceed with our plans for the new camp, sooner than we'd planned. Amelie threw herself into all things building and overseeing, and at the end of each day, she was spent. We both were. This was probably one of the most stressful times in both our lives. We were attempting to complete a project that would normally take a year in about half the time—simply so we could open that summer. Looking back, it was crazy. But it served its purpose. With a renewed sense of purpose, Amelie came out of her funk, for the most part, and I saw a side of her I'd never seen before. I saw a leader. And I fell more in love with her than I ever thought I could.

Seven months later, in early June, Camp Legacy II opened to its first visitors. Amelie taught photography and a class on poetry while I taught survival skills and ran the business side of things. In late August, Amelie handed me an envelope. It contained a black and white photograph of her hands resting on her abdomen holding a note that read, 'Finally.'

Shortly before Valentine's Day the following year, I held Amelie's hand as she pushed our daughter out into the world. We named her Evelyn, which means 'long-awaited child,' but also after the little girl Amelie had seen in the park the day she said the course of her future changed. Having a daughter is different from having a son, in the most difficult to explain way. In short, Evelyn was the most beautiful little thing I'd ever seen.

That is, until her sister, Sadie was born sixteen months later. Amelie and I didn't think she would get pregnant so easily—given the length of time it took us the first go round. But we were wrong.

By the time the girls were five and six respectively, they'd begun to ask why their parents weren't married the way their friend's parents were. So the following summer we said our 'I do's' in a small chapel we'd built on the camp property in front of Max and Molly, our daughters, and roughly two handfuls of people. It was the best day of our lives, we all agreed later.

And it was… then. But there would be other best days. And a few not so good ones, too. Which was ok. Because we had each other, and already, we'd learned a lot about surviving and getting through.

We found out that sometimes you wait seemingly forever

for something to happen—something that feels like it never would. But then it does—and it changes everything. And then from there—life has a way of just keeping on giving. *For better or worse.*

We learned that the wait is usually worth it—that good will come just as sure as the seasons change. We learned that happily(ish)-ever-afters do, in fact, exist. Even and *especially* when they take a while in the getting there.

Often the road ahead isn't clear. Life isn't a straight line from point A to point B. It's fraught with challenges and detours and things unforeseen. But most importantly, we learned that if you hang on, and you do your best to enjoy the ride—no matter how lost you get or how long the detour—you'll find you wind up where you were meant to be.

AFTERWORD

Dear Reader,

I hope you enjoyed reading my novel. Your engagement with my work means a great deal to me.

If it was your cup of tea, I'd be grateful if you'd consider leaving a review on Amazon.

Want to be the first to know when my next book is out? Sign up for my newsletter and never miss a release. (https://britneyking.com/newsletter/)

Thank you for your support—it truly means a lot to me.

And now, enjoy a sneak peek of another one of my books…

Britney King
Austin, Texas
November 2024

ABOUT THE AUTHOR

Britney King lives in Texas with her family, two literary dogs, one ridiculous cat, and a partridge in a pear tree.

When she's not wrangling the things mentioned above, she writes psychological, domestic, and romantic thrillers.

You can find Britney online here:

Web: https://britneyking.com
Facebook: https://www.facebook.com/BritneyKingAuthor
TikTok: https://www.tiktok.com/@britneyking_
Instagram: https://www.instagram.com/britneyking_/
BookBub: https://www.bookbub.com/authors/britney-king
Goodreads: https://bit.ly/BritneyKingGoodreads
Newsletter: https://britneyking.com/newsletter/

Want to make sure you never miss a release? Sign up for Britney's newsletter: https://britneyking.com/newsletter/

ACKNOWLEDGMENTS

Many thanks to my family and friends for your support in my creative endeavors.

To the beta team, ARC team, and the bloggers, thank you for making this gig so much fun.

Last, but not least, thank you for reading my work. Thanks for making this dream of mine come true.

I appreciate you.

ALSO BY BRITNEY KING

Standalone Novels

No Good Deed

I Said Run

Blood, Sweat, and Desire

The Sickness

Ringman

Good and Gone

Mail Order Bride

Fever Dream

The Secretary

Passerby

Kill Me Tomorrow

Savage Row

The Book Doctor

Room 553

HER

Around The Bend

Series

The Killer Series

Kill, Sleep, Repeat

Kill, Sleep, Repeat Volume II

The New Hope Series

The Social Affair / Book One

The Replacement Wife / Book Two

Speak of the Devil / Book Three

The New Hope Series Box Set

The Water Series

Water Under The Bridge / Book One

Dead In The Water / Book Two

Come Hell or High Water / Book Three

The Water Series Box Set

The Bedrock Series

Bedrock / Book One

Breaking Bedrock / Book Two

Beyond Bedrock / Book Three

The Bedrock Series Box Set

The With You Series

Somewhere With You / Book One

Anywhere With You / Book Two

The With You Series Box Set

SNEAK PEEK: AROUND THE BEND

If you were to pass me on the street, you probably wouldn't even look twice. I'm that normal. I'm just like you, only wealthier. I have it all. The kids, the family, the dog, a house on the hill. Hell—I'm so cliché, I even have a white picket fence. I guess you could say that I've dotted my I's and crossed my T's. But what I also have—what no one sees in yoga, or at Nieman Marcus, or during the dreadful Ladies Who Lunch charity events I attend (because only God knows why), and perhaps most importantly, in the school pick up line—are secrets.

Deep, dark, deadly secrets.

We all keep secrets, don't we? We all have thoughts in our heads, things we do, things about us that if people knew, they'd be shocked...right? Well, what if one day we just decided to let the cat out of the bag, so to speak.

What if we decided to let the whole world in on our dirty little secrets? And what if along the way, as we were spilling those secrets, we realized that things aren't always what they seem and with that knowledge, it changed the whole story? In this book, I'm laying it all out there. The unraveling of my life. My coming undone. What one might've seen had they been paying attention.

What I've found in life is people often believe lies before they'll believe the truth. Well, here it is, in a nutshell.

I'll let you decide which is which.

COPYRIGHT

Hot Banana Press
Cover Design by Britney King LLC
Cover Image by Mandy Hollis
Copy Editing by Literary Agent Rogena Mitchell-Jones
Proofread by Proofreading by the Page

First Edition: 2014
ISBN: 978-0-9892184-4-3 (Paperback)
ISBN: 978-0-9892184-5-0 (All E-Books)
britneyking.com

AROUND THE BEND

BRITNEY KING

To Jeremy, I miss you every day.
And to everyone who has ever loved someone through the pain.

CHAPTER ONE

EARLY SPRING

*N*ever assume things can't get worse. If you were to ask her what she'd learned over the past year, that's exactly what Jessica Clemens would have said. Well, that and more, but at the very least, this would, first and foremost, be it.

Things can always, always get worse.

Take for example the afternoon Jess was lounging in her sitting room pondering the shit-storm that had become her life when he, and by he, I'm referring to her husband Spencer, walked out of his closet, bags in hand.

This is how it all began. Her coming undone.

Truth be told, it began long before this. But that's the funny thing about stories, isn't it? It's hard to tell where the beginning and end are.

Now, had Jess been paying attention or hell, even been sober, she might have seen this coming. Alas, she did not.

And so, things did get worse from that moment on. Much, much worse.

That bright and cool spring afternoon, Spencer stood in front of his wife with a certain somber look on his face. It could have been remorse, she wasn't sure, for she was too high to tell the difference. The truth was, he had given Jess that look almost daily over the previous six months—so much so, she wasn't sure if it was her or if it had simply become his natural expression.

She glanced at him, down at his bags, and then cocked her brow. "I didn't know you had a trip this week," she said as she reached for her tumbler of vodka.

Spencer dropped the luggage and sat down on the foot-stool opposite her. "I'm fairly certain I told you…" He eyed her with pity, or perhaps anger, she couldn't gauge which. He started to speak again, but then paused before continuing. "You're looking a bit better today. And you're up." He smiled. "That's good news, isn't it?" He didn't wait for her to answer. "At any rate, I'm glad because we need to talk. This trip is going to be a bit of an extended one."

Jess eyed his bags again. "I can see that," she slurred tipping the glass in his direction.

He lowered his voice and spoke clearly, calmly—as though he were trying to talk her down from a ledge that she wasn't even aware she was hanging from. Jess knew better. She'd already fallen. "Jessica. Please. I know these past few months have been hard for you with the accident and all… and well, now this. But you need to understand that I'm not leaving for good. It'll only be a few weeks or so—a month max."

Had she been sober, she might have had the right mind to be angry, or to be hurt, or even devastated as she rightfully should've been. Instead, she found she was indifferent.

"Well… sayonara. And here's to you." She raised her glass,

then threw her head back and laughed. The man she'd loved for the past decade was, for the most part, walking out on her at a time when she clearly, really, *really* needed him, and she found it funny. That's how much trouble she was in. And Jess didn't even have the good sense to know it.

"Jessica." He reached for the tumbler, slid it forcefully from her hand, and placed it on the table. He stared at the glass as though he couldn't stand to look at her. "I need you to listen to what I'm trying to say here." He spoke, and then waited to ensure he had her attention before he continued. "I spoke to Addison at the agency a few moments ago. She's going to audit our staff and see what is needed in my absence. To start with, she's going to send someone over ASAP to help you get around a little more while I'm away..."

Jess scoffed. "You don't think we have enough help?"

"I don't want you to worry about anything." He took a deep breath and let it out. "Anyhow, about the children..."

"The children?" She interrupted defensively, even though the probability was low at that moment that she even had the prudence to consider the fact that they even had children. *That she had children.* That this would affect them.

"Yes, Jessica. Our children. Jonathan and Catherine..." He looked at the glass and back at her. "You do remember them, right?"

Jess sighed, picked up the glass, and finished it off. But she didn't take her eyes off his. Jess was a lot of things, but she wasn't dumb. She wouldn't admit defeat. "I'm not the one going on an extended vacation."

He raised his voice then. "This isn't a vacation, Jessica. This is business. And... quite frankly, I need to get away for a bit. I can't just sit around here twiddling my thumbs while my wife deteriorates into nothingness. Once again, you're not getting it." He paused, running his hands through his hair. Jess watched as his fingers slid slowly through his dark brown hair, which she'd always thought reminded her of smooth, silky chocolate, and wondered just how long it had been since she'd done the same.

"We've been over and over this... I'm not sure how else to say it. I need to give you some space to handle things on your own... Ever since the accident, well, I think you've forgotten who you are. While I'm gone, I want you to focus on getting back to your old self. I figure the only way you'll do that is if I force your hand."

Jess glanced toward the door and back at her husband. "So what are you waiting for then?"

She watched as he took one last look at her, stood, and walked out, all straight-backed and righteous. But all she could think about at that moment was what the women at the Ladies Who Lunch event would say the following day and every day after that. Because Jess, as drunk and high as she might have been, realized more than her husband did that afternoon. He was never coming back. Not really, anyway.

∾

READ MORE HERE: https://books2read.com/ aroundthebend